MASSACRE AT EMPIRE FASTNESS

Butch Shilton and Joe Peters are both out of work when fate deals them a ten-year stretch in prison. But they soon find themselves the only survivors of the massacre at Empire Fastness Way Station and they set out to track down the killers. However, Butch and Joe are accused of the massacre, and, faced with a posse on their trail and the killers of Empire Fastness Way Station hunting them down, their chances of survival are slim . . .

P. McCORMAC

MASSACRE AT EMPIRE FASTNESS

Complete and Unabridged

LINFORD
Leicester

First published in Great Britain in 2007 by
Robert Hale Limited
London

First Linford Edition
published 2008
by arrangement with
Robert Hale Limited
London

British Library CIP Data

McCormac, P.
   Massacre at Empire Fastness.—
   Large print ed.—
   Linford western library
   1. Western stories
   2. Large type books
   I. Title
   823.9′2 [F]

ISBN 978–1–84782–356–4

Published by
F. A. Thorpe (Publishing)
Anstey, Leicestershire

Set by Words & Graphics Ltd.
Anstey, Leicestershire
Printed and bound in Great Britain by
T. J. International Ltd., Padstow, Cornwall

This book is printed on acid-free paper

For John Auerbach and P.J. Gilbert

I count myself in nothing else so
   happy.
As a soul remembering my good
   friends.

Richard II Shakespeare

1

Butch Shilton hung by his fingertips from the window ledge. Above him he could hear a querulous voice.

'Someone been here, you slut. Tell me or I'll beat the living daylights outta you.'

'Geoff Pleasance, you couldn't beat your way out of a sugar bag,' a woman's voice answered. 'You touch me and you'll regret it. I'll tear your eyes outta your miserable skull so as you won't be able to count all that money you been hoarding. When you gonna give me the money for a new dress, or at least a new hat?'

Butch cursed silently. His fingers were aching as he hung desperately to the window ledge. He scrabbled urgently with his feet trying to find a toehold to relieve the agony in his wrists and fingers. To add to his

1

discomfort he was stark naked. A cold breeze was blowing across his naked body and the goose bumps stood out on his knotted muscles.

Butch was a down-at-heel cowboy. Compactly built he had a strong muscled body, which stood him in good stead now as he clung like a barnacle to the side of the building that was the home of Judge Pleasance.

Eleanor Pleasance was years younger than her ageing husband. Early in her marriage she had discovered that being the wife of a wealthy judge did not ensure a life of opulence. The judge kept his wealth locked away and spent nothing on his frivolous, young wife. His idea of a good time was a round of bridge with his avaricious family who lusted after his wealth and his young wife with equal enthusiasm.

Butch had been a willing visitor to Eleanor's bedroom. His interest in her was purely physical. They had been indulging in an evening of pleasure when the judge had arrived home unexpectedly. The cowboy had flung his clothes, along with his boots, out of the window and followed them with the intention of escaping the house when he discovered he was a considerable distance from the ground. Hence he was clinging desperately to the window ledge and praying the judge would go back to wherever he had so inconveniently appeared from.

'It's bitterly cold in here. Shut that goddamn window.'

The judge's words did indeed freeze Butch against the side of the building.'

'I need the fresh air,' snapped Eleanor.

'Fresh air, my ass.'

The footsteps approached the window and stopped.

'What the hell! Them's goddamn fingers!'

A face appeared out the window and stared down at Butch.

'Howdy, Judge. I told my friends I could climb up any building just like a spider. They bet me I couldn't climb up your wall. I guess I won the bet, eh?'

'Goddamn! Goddamn!' The judge began to hammer on Butch's fingers. 'Goddamn you to hell!'

'No . . . ' yelled Butch, 'you don't understand!'

'Stop it, you old fool, you'll kill him.'

It was Eleanor joining in. She wrapped her arms around the judge's neck and tried to pull him away from the window. It was too late. There was a scream from outside and then a solid thump as a body hit the ground several yards below.

Eleanor screamed also and the judge slammed shut the window. He hurried from the bedroom. In the hallway he retrieved an ancient shotgun and cautiously peered outside. His wife was still screaming as he stepped out onto the porch.

★ ★ ★

'Raise two dollars and bet another three.'

Joe Peters stared at the three tens in

his hand and silently contemplated his options. He had started the game with his last ten dollars with the intention of increasing his fortune. Now he was down to four dollars. To stay in the game he would have to use up the last of his cash.

'Come on, fella, we ain't got all night,' grumbled the man across the table from Joe.

The gambler was a clean-shaven young man with shifty eyes. He wore a shabby derby that he was in the habit of removing and using the kerchief he kept stored inside the hat to mop his forehead.

'Look, fella,' Joe replied, 'when you're down to your last few dollars you takes your time.'

'Damn greenhorns, if you don't know how to play poker you shouldn't be in the game.'

As he spoke, he removed his derby and began the ritual of wiping. Joe was glowering at the gambler from under lowered lids. It was because the gambler thought Joe was absorbed in his cards that he was careless. It was pure fluke Joe saw the card being slipped on to the table. The ritual with the hat, the kerchief and the head wiping suddenly became clear. Joe pursed his lips thoughtfully and then slowly pushed his last few dollars into the pile in the middle of the table.

'I'll see you, fella.'

There was a smirk of triumph on the gambler's face as he laid his cards out. 'Four kings; looks as if you've had a bad run of luck, greenhorn.'

The gambler was openly sneering at the big man sitting across the table. That Joe Peters was a tenderfoot was obvious from his store-bought clothes. Back in Bosworth he had served as a cabinet-maker working for a man who taught him all his skills. Joe had fallen in love with his master's daughter, Eliza Wardell. They had married in the fall. Before they married Joe had revealed to Eliza his dreams of establishing his own business.

'There is a mass exodus of settlers moving out West. Just think of the building work that must be going on to accommodate this new populace. Every fresh building must have furniture and fittings. There'll be work to keep me so busy I'll be able to employ several tradesmen.'

Before they could make the move Eliza had become pregnant. Rather than expose his young family to the rigors of the trek, Joe had decided to go it alone and get established before sending for them. It had all started to go wrong at Hinkly.

The frenzy of activity was as he imagined it. The smell of sawdust was like a fog hanging over the turmoil of the building work. Inhabitants of the new town woke in the morning to the pounding of hammers. At night they were lulled to sleep by the murmur of carpenters' saws.

He had not been in the town long before his tools were stolen. Joe had trudged from building site to building site explaining his plight. It was all to no avail. Without his tools Joe was just another labourer seeking a job in an industry overburdened with cheap workers. The story was the same everywhere he went.

'Sorry, fella, could do with a good carpenter but we need men with their own tools. Come back in a week.'

Joe was almost destitute and the only solution he could envisage was to win enough at cards to buy tools in order to ply his trade.

Gambling houses and saloons had sprung up almost overnight. Builders, farmers and cowmen working all day, needed to relax and there were men and women willing to provide the entertainment who were skilled at extracting money from the gullible. Joe realized he had been set up. His last few dollars were residing in the pocket of the cheap tinhorn gambler sneering at him from across the table.

2

The judge heard a noise in the dark and swung around towards the sound. The twin barrels of his shotgun were held out before him like accusing fingers. A pale, ghost-like form was limping painfully slowly towards the front gate.

'Stop at once, you goddamn blackguard. Stop or I shoot!'

The dim silhouette began to limp faster. Judge Pleasance pulled the trigger. A deafening report blasted out into the quiet of the night. Flame lanced from the barrel of the gun. There was a scream and the figure tumbled to the ground and writhed around in agony.

'Goddamn it, I warned you.'

The judge advanced cautiously towards the groaning man lying in his front garden.

'What the hell's going on there?' someone yelled from the road.

'Come on up here and help me,' the judge yelled back. 'I caught me a varmint.'

Two men came warily up to the front gate, 'What's going on, Judge?' Seeing the groaning man they moved inside the garden. 'What the hell! Why's he got no clothes on?'

'Danged if I know,' answered the judge. 'Maybe he thought to slide through my windows easier with no clothes to snag.' The judge kept his weapon trained on the injured man. He reached over and gingerly poked the groaning man. 'That was rock salt I peppered you with, mister. This other barrel is loaded with lead shot. You come easy and you might just survive this night.'

'Oh God, my ass is on fire,' moaned the injured man. 'I'll come easy, fella. Just point that shotgun a little to the right.' Butch Shilton tried to sit up in and moaned piteously.

'We'll take him down the jail, Judge Pleasance. You run and fetch Sheriff

Patterson. He's usually to be found down in the Bounty Saloon this time of the night.'

'I know rightly where the sheriff spends his evenings,' replied the judge testily. 'You want this shotgun?'

'Nah, he don't look like he'll be much trouble.'

'Well, just you make sure you get him safely to the jail.'

'I don't think I can walk. My leg must be broke.' Butch had managed to get to his knees. 'Help me with these britches,' he pleaded.

★ ★ ★

A big, work-hardened hand clamped down on the gambler's wrist as he reached for the winnings.

'What the hell, greenhorn!' the man snarled, as he looked up into the pleasant, smiling face of Joe Peters. 'You're hurting my arm, damn you.'

'Not as much as you hurt my pocket,' said Joe amiably.

Still holding tight to the wrist he dragged the man towards him. The gambler struggled wildly as he was pulled on to the top of the table.

'Goddamn you, I'll kill you for this, you piss-ass loser. Lemme go!'

When he had his victim helpless on the table Joe reached out with his other hand and removed the man's derby. He slapped the hat on the table and the hidden cards flopped out for all to see. The other men at the table gasped.

'Well I'll be! Goddamn tinhorn gambler. Look at that. Hid the cards in his hat.'

Joe had a grim look on his face as he retained his hold on his victim. 'I guess I'll take my money back, mister.' He scooped the pot from the table and stuffed the money in his pocket.

'I was only joshing you, fella,' the tinhorn whined. 'I woulda let you have the money back anytime. Now let me go. You're near to busting my goddamn arm.'

Joe reached into the tinhorn's pocket

and extracted a wad of bills. He tossed this to the table. 'There you are, fellas, you heard the gent. He wants to give us back our money. Count me out ten dollars and divide the rest amongst yourselves.'

'Some of that money's mine, you gumball,' shrieked the gambler. Spit flew from his lips as he glared angrily at his tormentor.

The men at the table fell gleefully to the task of dividing up the sudden bounty.

'Maybe these fellas might let you play a little poker to get it back again,' Joe said mildly. 'If I was you I'd watch out for cheats. Seems to me this town is filled with thieves and vagabonds. Just be careful who you play with in future.'

With the money divvied up, Joe let go the gambler's wrist and pocketed the rest of his money. It had been a disappointing result to his night of speculation, but at least he had ended up none the worse from his experience. If anything he was a little wiser.

" 'Night, gents,' he said as he turned to go.

'Watch out!'

Joe swung back at the shouted warning. The gambler was levelling a small derringer and there was a triumphant glint in his mean eyes. For a big man Joe could move quickly. Even as the little gun spat out its slug Joe was grasping the edge of the table. He felt a sharp blow on his shoulder. Ignoring the sudden pain from the bullet he heaved hard at the table. At the same time he rammed forward. The table edge caught the gambler's midriff. He yelled as the table slammed him backwards.

Joe flung the table effortlessly from him. The gambler was scrambling to get away. He stood no chance as the big man caught up with him. Joe was moving fast as he scooped up the smaller man. Holding him by jacket and pants seat he kept up his momentum and rammed the gambler head first into the wall. The gambler's

14

screams were cut short as his head hit the solid obstruction. Effortlessly, Joe dragged the man back from the wall and rammed forward again. There was a sickening crack as the man's vertebrae fractured. Suddenly men were grabbing at Joe and trying to pull him back.

'You gonna kill that tinhorn. For Gawd's sake let go.'

It took four of them to pull the cabinet-maker away from the limp form of the gambler. Joe was breathing hard. His arm was hurting where the gambler had shot him.

'Mind my goddamn arm,' he protested.

There was a click and Joe felt something hard and round poke into his neck.

'OK, fella, ease up, or I'll blow your goddamn head off.'

Joe went still. A tall narrow-shouldered man stood beside him holding a Remington pistol. He was wearing a lawman's badge.

'You fellas,' — the sheriff indicated

the men holding Joe — 'hold tight to that man till he cools off.'

'Sheriff, this one's dead. The tin-horn's dead.'

Sheriff Patterson looked down at the man kneeling by the inert form of the gambler. The sheriff turned back to the men pinioning Joe. 'Take him down the jail. You're in trouble, fella. We don't stand for murder in this here town.'

3

The courtroom was crowded. The circumstances of the crimes of the accused had circulated widely around town. The story went that Butch Shilton had been apprehended at Judge Pleasance's house. A seemingly incredible part of the tale was that he was naked at the time of his arrest. Speculation ran high as to his intentions.

Butch was well known in the district as a womanizer. Married or single it was all the same to Butch Shilton. That Eleanor Pleasance was much younger than the judge caused the gossips to nod knowingly. They were eager to be in at the hearing. Spicy details from this case could not be learned second-hand. The gossips and the nosy parkers crowded the courtroom.

The killing at the saloon was not so

unique as to bring in such a large crowd. Nevertheless the circumstances surrounding the incident were cause for speculation. There was not much sympathy for the victim.

'That tinhorn gambler deserved all he got.'

'Allus wondered how so he managed to win so often. Hid the cards inside his hat as I heard it.'

'The guy as done it was a giant of a fella.'

'No he weren't. He were a big fella to be sure, but he weren't no giant.'

'Waal, he did kill that tinhorn with his bare hands. Picked him up and snapped his neck like a rotten stick.'

'Lucky for us the sheriff was there and arrested him afore he could go on the rampage. Way I heard it he murdered all his family back East and was on the run from the law.'

'What — murdered his own darn family?'

'Sure thing; strangled them all with his bare hands — his wife and kids and her mother and father. Seven as what I heard it.'

In both cases the stories grew and were embroidered upon. The legend of a ruthless, murdering monster from back East was being born.

Butch Shilton became, in the citizens' imagination, a lurid pervert who danced naked through the streets. No woman of any age was safe from him.

'All stand for the judge.'

Judge Pleasance entered in top hat and morning coat. He took his seat at the dais and removed his headgear.

'Humph!' He glared sourly around at the crowded court. 'Ain't you folk got anything more important to do than sit and gawk at courtroom cases?'

'We come to see justice done, Judge.'

'Sure thing, Judge, we expect to see the wisdom of Solomon and the justice of Judge Pleasance.'

'Hang them fellas, Judge. We ain't had a hanging in weeks.'

There were hoots of laughter around the courtroom as these pleasantries were bandied about.

'Silence!'

To emphasize his order the judge hammered on the table with the heel of an old clog. The antique piece of wooden footwear had been introduced by Judge Pleasance half in jest.

'The sure boot of justice will stamp down on any wrong-doing in this here community,' he had stated when he had first used the wooden clog in the courtroom. 'Justice is a boot that'll kick the criminal classes outta Hinkly.'

Judge Pleasance glared belligerently around the room.

'Any more noise an' I'll clear the court.'

There was a shuffling and a muted muttering in the crowded courtroom but no more interruptions. No one wanted to risk being ejected for fear of missing anything concerning the two criminals.

The judge grunted with ill-tempered humour then shuffled some papers before him while he waited to see if his warning was to be heeded. Satisfied he had quelled any unrest, he looked up eventually with an irascible scowl on his face.

'Bring in the first defendant.'

Two deputies helped Butch Shilton in. He was limping badly but this did not prevent him from grinning broadly at the people in the courtroom. One or two called greetings, for Butch was well known in Hinkly and well liked. Judge Pleasance rapped sharply with the quaint piece of footwear.

'No communication with the prisoner!' he barked testily.

There was immediate silence. At a nod from the judge, Sheriff Patterson rose to his feet. He had a sheet of paper in his hand from which he read the charges.

'Butch Shilton herewith is charged with burglary, assault, attempted murder, resisting arrest, indecent behaviour, causing a fracas, civic disorder, vagrancy.'

'Hell, Judge, I never done all those

things the sheriff just said as I did. As I told you at the time I made a bet with these fellas that I could climb up any tree or building. They challenged me to climb up the side of a house. Your house just happened to be handy so I shinned up like a squirrel. I've often been likened to a squirrel for my climbing abilities.'

'Humph!' snorted the judge. 'So you just took off all your clothes and climbed my house to rob what you could?'

'Hell, no, Judge, I took my clothes off as that way I don't snag anything.'

'You was naked so as you could get in where the judge couldn't,' an anonymous voice called out.

There were hoots of laughter from the crowd. The judge's face grew red. He hammered hard with his wooden clog.

'Silence! Goddamn silence in court! Sheriff Patterson — arrest that person.'

Sheriff Patterson looked uncertainly into the mob of chortling citizens. 'Step up the fella as just shouted out. Don't you know you're in contempt of court?'

The laughter was gradually dying down.

'Do your job and arrest that varmint, Sheriff,' snarled the judge.

The sheriff shrugged helplessly in his direction. 'Hell, Judge Pleasance, I don't rightly know who to arrest. Nobody's owned up.'

The judge glared round the courtroom. 'Next time anyone interrupts I'll fine the whole goddamn lot of you.' He shuffled his papers. 'Call witness for prosecution.'

The witnesses for the prosecution were the judge's neighbours who had come to his rescue the previous night after they heard the discharge from the scattergun. There was no doubt in their minds that Butch was up to no good. They caught him trying to escape from the judge's front garden and verified the fact that he was indeed stark naked.

'Witness for the defence,' the judge growled, at the end of this evidence.

Butch stood straighter in the dock. 'Judge, I ain't got no witnesses. The fellas as challenged me to climb up a house all refuse to testify.'

'They refuse because there ain't no such fellas,' came the sharp reply from the judge.

'It's like this, your honour, them fellas bet me a considerable amount of money on the dare. Now if they come forward, they has to honour the bet. They're a bunch of lying, thieving, low-down bottom feeders,' Butch asserted vehemently.

Judge Pleasance stared shrewdly at Butch. 'Mr Shilton, you name those fellas as is your witnesses and I'll swear out an affidavit for their appearance in this here court. Then they'll have to witness or they'll end up in the dock alongside you.'

Butch Shilton's mouth opened and closed a few times as he thought over the judge's words. Well known as a man who was never stuck for something to say, it seemed he was speechless now.

'Well, speak up. I can't hear a word you're saying.' Judge Pleasance cocked his head towards the prisoner and cupped his hand behind his ear while at the same time screwing up his face as if straining to listen.

'Judge, them fellas are slippery as eels. The whole lotta them there pack rats lit outta town as soon as they knew I was in jail. They musta knowed about that there Abby Davis you was gonna set on them. You let me outta this here court and I'll track them double-crossing crawlbellies and bring them back here for to testify.'

A sly smile crossed Judge Pleasance's face. 'You know what I think, son, you ain't got no witnesses? Which means you just committed perjury. I'm adding that to the list of charges against you.' He shifted needlessly through the papers in front of him. 'My, my, my, my, Mr Shilton — burglary, assault, attempted murder, resisting arrest, indecent behaviour, causing a fracas, civic disorder, vagrancy and now perjury. It appears you are a very dangerous man, Mr Butch Shilton. Too dangerous to be allowed to roam free to prey on innocent citizens. I sentence you to ten years' hard labour in the state penitentiary.'

There was a stunned silence in the court.

'Sheriff Patterson, take the prisoner back to the cells where he can await transport to his new home.'

'Godaamn it, Judge, you can't do this to me!'

But Butch's protests were cut short as the deputies hauled him unceremoniously from the dock.

'Judge Pleasance, goddamn it to hell . . . ' Butch's remonstrations were becoming indistinct as he was dragged from the courtroom.

There was a satisfied smirk on Judge Pleasance's face as he listened to the fading yells of Butch Shilton.

'Next prisoner.'

4

Butch regarded his fellow prisoner with some interest. He was a big, well-built man with muscular shoulders and arms. 'What you in for, fella?'

Joe Peters looked across at the man in the adjoining cell. Butch was resting with his back against the bars of his prison. Joe wondered why the fellow did not sit on the bunk as he was doing himself. He was leaning at an angle. His foot was resting on a rolled up blanket he had placed on the floor nearby.

'Killed a fella — a tinhorn gambler.'

Butch regarded the big man curiously. 'What did the judge give you?'

Joe sighed deeply. 'Goddamn ten years' hard labour.'

'You too!' Butch exclaimed. 'He sentenced me to the same ten years' hard labour. Looks like we might be seeing a lot of each other. Name's Butch Shilton.'

'Howdy Butch, Joe Peters.' His curiosity got the better of him. 'I ain't ever seen you sit. You gotta problem with sitting?'

'Damn judge put a load of buckshot into my ass,' Butch replied ruefully. 'Well, it weren't buckshot but rock salt.' Butch eased into a more comfortable position.

'The judge shot you — what were you doing?'

A slow smile crossed Butch's face. 'I was pleasuring the judge's wife when he come home unannounced.' The smile slowly faded. 'Damn me, it were good, but it weren't worth ten years of a man's life!'

'I take it you're not married then?'

'Married!' Butch shot his fellow prisoner a disgusted look. 'In my book marriage is a millstone around a fella's neck. I believe in the old adage: there's safety in numbers. The more women I have the safer I am from the malady of matrimony. What about you? You ever tie the knot?'

Joe Peters sighed deeply and stared down at his clenched hands. 'Yeah, married last year back in Bosworth. Was hoping to come out here with my wife. Then she was pregnant. Didn't want to bring her out here till I had established a place for her and me and the babe.' He shook his head dolefully. 'Sure glad I didn't bring her with me. I was seeking work as a carpenter but then my tools were stolen. Thought I'd win money at gambling to buy some more tools. That tinhorn was fleecing me. We got in a fight and now I'm here with a ten-year stretch ahead of me.'

'Man, that is bad luck. Have you writ your wife to tell her the bad news?'

Joe shook his head. 'I ain't gonna tell her. No use worrying her. I'll just have to disappear. She'll never know what a mess I made of things.' He looked up at Butch. 'What about you? You got any family?'

Butch shook his head. 'I have family

somewheres but they won't miss me.'

The prisoners fell into an uneasy silence as both contemplated their future.

'Goddamn it I'll be an old man when I come out of the pen.'

They looked at each other with some concern.

'The best years of our life,' Butch mused, as he shifted into a more comfortable position.

Joe noticed his companion favoured his leg. 'You got something the matter with your leg?'

Butch looked down ruefully at the foot he was resting on his makeshift pad.

'Hadda jump outta the judge's window when he arrived. Goddamn bust my leg some. Then the judge goes and blows away my ass.'

'You can hardly blame him. After all, it was his wife you were humping. Come to think about it, that judge is an old fella. What were you doing with his wife? You some kinda gigolo?'

'Hell no! She's a young bird. She only married the judge for his money. Wanted a bit of fun.' Butch stuck out his chest and a smug look appeared on his face. 'Naturally she chose me.'

'Well, maybe this'll teach you to leave other men's wives alone in future,' Joe observed.

'Don't matter two hoots now. Looks like I'm gonna spend the rest of my life with a bunch of jailbirds.'

The rattle of keys and movement from the main part of the building drew their attention. A portly young man came through accompanied by an older man in his fifties. The younger man nodded at Butch. He had a dark goatee beard and moustache.

'Howdy, Butch, sure sorry about all this but I drew the short straw to escort you and this killer to the penitentiary.'

'Howdy, Gordon. I guess someone hasta do it.'

'My uncle John, he's coming along to help me.' Gordon jerked a thumb at the older man.

Like his nephew John Biddell was chubby. He nodded sourly at the prisoner but said nothing. Gordon unlocked the cell and held out a pair of handcuffs almost apologetically.

'Gotta put these on, Butch.'

Once manacled, Butch hobbled out of his cell.

'Watch this one, Uncle John,' Gordon said, as he unlocked Joe's cell. 'He's that crazy killer from back East.'

Obediently, Uncle John pulled his pistol and trained it on Joe. 'Don't worry, Gordon, he makes a wrong move and we'll be planting him in boot hill. He won't ever make it to the pen.'

'What about breakfast, Gordon?' Butch queried, as he watched Joe being handcuffed. 'I sure could eat a big breakfast right now. My belly's acting like a snapping turtle.'

'Sorry, Butch, no food. Sheriff Patterson's idea. He reckons hungry prisoners is more unlikely to cause trouble.'

'Hell dang Sheriff Patterson! It's his

bounden duty to feed us. More'n likely he's putting the money to feed us in his own pocket. Whatever happened to justice in this country? I get a load of trumped-up charges agin me. Judge Pleasance shoots me and nobody asks for him to be put on trial for attempted murder, and now the law wants to starve me. As soon as I gets the chance I'm writing to Congress to complain about the state of injustice in this here town.'

'All right now, Butch, the horses are saddled up outside ready and waiting.'

Butch's eyes widened as a thought struck him. 'Gordon, I ain't fit to sit in no saddle. My ass is raw as a scraped carrot. I ain't sat on anything since Judge Pleasance shot me.'

The deputy looked as distressed as his prisoner. 'Maybe we can get you a cushion or something, Butch. I'll ask the sheriff.'

Sheriff Patterson, as befits a man with his hard reputation, was unsympathetic. 'Butch, you shoulda thought about that afore you went crawling around people's houses naked. I been assigned one horse to transport you. Now you can sit on that mare, or you can lie on that mare, or you can be dragged behind that mare. I don't give a hangman's cuss what you do. Deputy Biddle, take these goddamn prisoners outta here and carry out your orders.'

In the end a bedroll was wedged in front of the saddle so that Butch could lie forward on the horse with his backside hiked in the air.

Before they could start out there was a sudden yell from the sheriff's office and Sheriff Patterson appeared in the doorway glowering at his two deputies.

'Gordon, what the hell's going on there?'

'Just getting the prisoners ready for the journey, sir,' Gordon stuttered.

Sheriff Patterson's face tightened. 'Damn it, Gordon, I don't rightly know why I appointed you deputy. It was against my better judgement. Only I owed your uncle, or I would never have allowed it. Get your ass over here.'

The sheriff and his deputy disappeared inside the building. In a very short time Gordon appeared looking rather crestfallen.

'Sheriff reckons he's gonna make the trip himself.'

Sheriff Patterson pushed past his deputy. Around the lawman's waist was strapped a gunbelt with twin holsters holding matched Remington double-action revolvers. Before he reached the horse he bent and tied down the holsters.

'Goddamn want a job done gotta do it your goddamn self,' he muttered. 'Gordon, you look after the store. Anyone gives you trouble just shoot them, or throw them in jail.'

As he boarded his mount he looked askance at the strange posture of his prisoner. With a wicked grin on his face he reached out with his reins and slashed Butch across his elevated rear end. Two things happened: Butch shrieked in agony and his mount took off along the street in a wild gallop.

'Come on, Uncle John,' the sheriff called out gleefully, as he urged his own mount in pursuit. 'Looks like Butch is real anxious to get to that there prison.'

5

The way station was a huddle of log cabins. A combined bar and eating-place was the main attraction where thirsty and hungry travellers could buy home-brewed alcohol and mouldering victuals. Another cabin was given over to rows of louse-infested bunks where those same travellers could stay the night. Stables and a corral contained a motley collection of nags for sale or hire. Dilapidated buggies and wagons were parked in the weed-filled yard. These rickety vehicles could also be traded for.

A stage came through every three days carrying mail and passengers. This was a stop for the stage line where the driver changed his team of horses and the passengers could take a break from the bone jarring journey over deep-rutted roads.

'There she lies,' Sheriff Patterson observed. 'Empire Fastness Way Station. Lousy beer, lousy grub and lousy accommodation. I guess we all need a break from all this travelling. What do you say, Butch?'

After three days of riding Butch had begun the process of healing. By padding his saddle with his blanket he could now ride in the normal fashion. The time on top of his horse had also allowed the swelling in his leg to subside. When he first tumbled from the upper window of the judge's house he feared it had been broken. At night when they stopped to camp he found he could walk with reasonable confidence on the injured leg. Now his brain was working overtime on plans of escape.

'Sheriff, when you gonna let us have some grub?' he complained bitterly.

During their trek Sheriff Patterson had resolutely refused to feed the prisoners. He turned in his saddle and regarded Butch with some amusement.

'Butch, I figure you don't realize I'm doing you a favour. From what I know of prison food most folk wouldn't feed it to a hog. Just to throw you straight in that place after eating Uncle John's home cooking would be plain cruelty. This way, by the time we get you to that there penitentiary you'll be so hungry, if they offered you fried buffalo chips you'd be so glad you'd eat everything put in front of you and ask for more. So stop moaning about grub and just be grateful I've got such a kind, considerate nature.'

'Hell, Sheriff, I might never last that long. I'll just fall off this nag and die of starvation. When that happens don't take my body on to the state penitentiary. Just bury me by the trail and put up a grave marker.'

'Butch Shilton,' mused the sheriff, 'topped the judge's wife and then toppled from his horse. How's that for a epitaph.'

Butch shot a baleful look back at the lawman. 'Starved to death by Sheriff

Patterson would be more fitting.'

Chortling quietly to himself the sheriff led the little party down towards Empire Fastness Way Station.

A fat greasy man was installed behind the bar. His shirt was open to the navel exposing sagging breasts and a swelling expanse of belly that was in the process of pushing his trousers towards his boots.

'Welcome, welcome.' His grin of welcome faded somewhat as he noted the lawman's badge.

'You gotta root cellar here?'

The eyes became wary. 'Root cellar? Sure thing, but I never use it. The place is infested with rodents.' The owner of the way station was wary of the question for the root cellar was where he brewed his illicit liquor.

'Rodents you say? Even better. Got two prisoners with me. Your root cellar secure?'

'I . . . I think so.'

'Much obliged for the use of it for one night.'

40

'Is more comfortable in the dormitory,' ventured the keeper.

Sheriff Patterson shook his head. 'It's not comfort I'm after. The more uncomfortable the better. That rodent-infested cellar sounds just the place.'

The sheriff returned outside where his deputy was watching over his two charges.

'Gentlemen, I got good news. We got first-class accommodation arranged.'

Behind the station they found heavy wooden doors at ground level held in place by a sturdy padlock. The keeper was there ahead of them, opening up. His grin was sickly as he watched the sheriff push his protesting prisoners into the dark interior. The doors were slammed shut. Butch Shilton and Joe Peters found themselves inside a totally black hole that reeked like a cesspit. Ignoring the yells of protest from Butch, the sheriff and his deputy retired to the bar for refreshments and eats.

'Joe, I been in some holes but this

beats all other holes into a steer's backside.'

The root cellar was nothing more than a pit dug into the ground with a wooden trapdoor to keep it secure. Cautiously they felt their way around their dungeon. At the rear of their tomb they found a collection of barrels. Butch rapped on a barrel with his knuckles.

'Joe, will you pinch me? I wanna know if lack of food has caused me to hallucinate. Have we or have we not landed ourselves into a brewery?'

Joe could hear banging and gurgling noises as his companion explored further. Suddenly a large jug was pushed into his hand.

'Try a taste of that.'

Joe sniffed cautiously. 'Well, it might be beer — then again it might be buffalo urine.'

Butch chuckled. 'You could be right. I reckon I've drunk similar stuff in the past. What the hell, I'm gonna get drunk outta my brain.' There was the burble of someone drinking deeply. 'When Sheriff Patterson comes to collect us in the morning I reckon to be totally insensible. He'll have to rope me in that there saddle.'

Butch could feel his stomach gurgling unpleasantly as the raw liquor swilled into his empty innards. He burped loudly. Beside him Joe sipped cautiously.

'It might go to our heads on an empty stomach,' Joe observed.

The slurping noises from his companion continued unabated.

'Aaah. Happy are they in cellars for they shall inherit the root beer.'

6

The sun came up bright and early, bathing the way station in a harsh white light. It had the promise of being a blisteringly hot day. Sheriff Patterson groaned and tried to open his eyes. His stomach grumbled unpleasantly and he felt the stirrings of his bowels. He sat up in the bunk and saw his deputy wide-awake and staring at him from the next bunk.

'Goddamn, what the hell that fella puts in that beer of his? I guess some of that rat poison he uses in his root cellar musta got in the brew. I feel like my stomach wants to claw its way outta my ass.' He groaned loudly. 'I'm getting too old for this. The only reason I took on this mission was to see my cousin Jim Slater what's governor at the prison.'

He rolled out of the bunk and, scratching furiously, disappeared out

44

the back door. The deputy sat up, yawned, stretched and scratched. Then he followed his boss outside.

The lawmen were at breakfast when they heard the horses approaching. Sheriff Patterson had prodded at the stodgy beans before pushing his plate to one side and with a look of distaste sipped at the vile-tasting dark brew the owner assured him was coffee.

As far as the sheriff could tell they were the only customers. A fat Indian woman worked in the kitchen while a young half-breed girl with vacant eyes and slovenly dress and manners served at tables. Before they retired for the night the proprietor had offered the women to the two lawmen for a modest sum.

'One is my wife and the other my daughter. They will make your bed warm for you.'

Sheriff Patterson had been tempted to send the women to entertain the prisoners incarcerated in the root cellar. As it was he declined all offers and the prisoners were left to contemplate their fate alone and in the dark.

Outside they could hear horses pull into the yard. The sheriff idly watched the door. To the background noises of blowing horses and jingling harness a gaunt elderly man stepped inside and stood to one side of the door. For a long moment he surveyed the room. He had deep-set eyes like pieces of agate embedded in his skull. His lower face was covered with an unkempt greying beard. A wide-brimmed hat shaded his face.

For no reason he could place, Sheriff Patterson felt a tiny shiver of apprehension along his spine.

'Welcome, welcome my friend,' the fat man behind the bar called.

Only then did the gaunt man move towards the bar. One by one the rest of his crew followed. As each of the other four men stepped inside the room the sheriff's disquiet grew.

Unaware of the tension growing in his boss, Uncle John worked steadily at the unappetizing mess of beans — from time to time slurping noisily from the tin mug of foul-tasting coffee.

The old man's four companions were all much younger men. Two of them sauntered to a table behind the sheriff and straddled chairs. The other two joined the old man at the bar and placed themselves each side of him facing into the room. They stared unblinking at the lawmen. They had the same cold, cruel expressions as the old man.

The fat man behind the bar slid tin mugs in front of his new customers. There was a slight tremor in his hand as he picked up an earthenware jug.

'Good homebrew, gentlemen.'

'When's the stage due?'

The man's voice was soft and throaty. It reminded Sheriff Patterson of a wind searching the cracks of a deserted house.

'Stage? Should be along anytime now. Can I fix you breakfast while you wait?' The tremor in the fat man's hand had transferred itself to his voice.

'Dave, watch outside for the stage.'

The man to the left of the leader turned and took the jug from the unresisting hand of the barkeep. He was at least six feet tall and lean with a slightly rounded boyish face. Without a word he strode to the door and went outside.

The gaunt man turned his attention to the lawmen. Slowly he appraised the two men and then tramped across to stand before their table.

'You looking for someone, Marshal?'

In spite of his anxiety about these men Sheriff Patterson was not a man to be cowed easy. He eased back in his chair, very conscious of the weight of the twin Remington pistols nestling in their holsters. Casually his hands dropped to his lap.

'What's it to you, fella?'

He did not think it worthwhile to point out that he was a sheriff and not a marshal. The face before him was lipless; there was a gash where lips would have hung.

'Just curious, Marshal.'

It was a mistake to have forgotten the two men behind him. A wiry arm snapped around Patterson's neck and tightened hard against his throat. The sheriff grabbed at the arm. At the same time he kicked out with his heels and went backwards in his chair. The hold on his neck never slackened. Uncle John began to rise from his seat when he felt the pressure of a Colt against his temple.

'Just you carry on with your breakfast, fatty.'

With his deputy staring on, powerless to intervene, Sheriff Patterson was struggling helplessly against that strangling arm-lock. His eyes bulged and his mouth gaped open as he slowly choked. Desperately he clawed at that unyielding arm. It was like grappling with a tree root. His struggles grew feebler as the chokehold held fast. At last the old man lifted a hand and the pressure eased off.

Sheriff Patterson dragged in air, his mouth agape. During the brief, frantic struggle sweat had beaded on his forehead. He was sitting on the floor with his attacker squatting behind him and keeping his hold on him. Breathing hoarsely, he stared with hatred at the old man before him.

'I like polite people, Marshal. When I ask a question I expect an answer. Now just tell me what you're doing here.'

Breathing heavily the sheriff swallowed a few times before replying. 'Go to hell. My business is no concern of yours.'

The rigid limb around his neck began to tighten, but the old man again held up a hand. His eyes turned to the deputy. Uncle John was still sitting at the table. There was a frightened look on his podgy face as the gravity of their situation sank in.

'You the deputy?'

Uncle John nodded, his eyes wide with apprehension.

'Tell them nothing,' Sheriff Patterson

snarled, still defiant.

The arm tightened just enough to choke off any more speech.

'Where you from, fella?'

The deputy swallowed nervously. 'We're from Hinkly, just a few days' ride from here.'

'Who you trailing?'

'We ain't after no one, mister,' Uncle John stammered.

'What you doing here then?'

'We . . . we're after taking some prisoners to the penitentiary. Honest to God, mister, we ain't looking for no trouble.'

'The state pen,' mused the old man, nodding in satisfaction. The deputy was not to know the man interrogating him misinterpreted his answer. His understanding was that their mission complete, the lawmen were returning home. 'You see, the reason I asked was I thought you just might be after us. Not that we've ever done anything for the law to be going after us. It's just I got a suspicious mind. Lawmen have a

51

habit of thinking we're wrong 'uns.' He shook his head in regret. 'Can't be too cautious in a distrustful world like the one we live in.' Turning back to the fat owner of the way station he asked, 'What's in there?' He pointed to the door at the back of the room.

'I have bunks in there. You wanna stay the night I charge you a dollar, include meals.' He fixed a nervous smile on his features. 'Women are extra.'

The old man turned back to the lawmen. 'Take them in back. Find something to rope them to the bunks. Cut up sheets if you have to.'

'Please,' whined the sweating proprietor, 'do not cut up my bedding. I find you some rope.'

'You're overstepping the mark, fella,' the sheriff snarled, still defiant. 'Assaulting law officers and imprisoning them is a serious offence. If you ain't wanted by the law you surely will be now 'less you let us go right now and I might be persuaded to go lenient on you.'

A curt twist of the head and the

sheriff and his deputy were hustled from the room

'They give you any bother slit their throats. I want no shooting. We'll deal with them after the stage gets here.'

7

'Stage coming, Jabez.'

The six-footer had poked his head inside to give the warning. He blinked owlishly at his companions seated at the tables eating breakfast.

'You all eating while I havta stand outside in this consarned heat and keep a lookout,' he said plaintively.

'Dave, you had that there jug of homebrew for your breakfast. What more you want?'

The one who answered was the stocky youngster who had held Sheriff Patterson helpless in the neck-lock. The half-breed girl sat on his knee and he had his hand inside her buckskin top. The girl seemed in no way disturbed by the attention she was receiving. Her vacant eyes gazed into the distance. The youngster with the girl had taken off his hat exposing short, blond hair. Though he was not very tall he looked brutally strong with a barrel chest and muscular arms.

'Fellas, you know what to do.' The old man stood up as he spoke. He turned and addressed the way-station owner. 'Fat Man, what happens when the stage arrives?'

'The passengers come in here for refreshment while the driver changes the team.'

His agitation showed plainly on his chubby face. Sweat ran freely down his face and body and he mopped constantly with a dirty rag. It was the same cloth he used to wipe the grubby bar top and the vessels in which he served his dubious refreshments.

'Who gets the new team ready?'

'Usually my wife and daughter.'

'Right, tell them to get out there and get the team ready.'

'Sure thing, mister.'

The blond youngster had brushed the girl unceremoniously from him and was standing putting his hat in place.

'You like my daughter, kid?' the barkeep asked, then wished he hadn't.

Small, dark, mean eyes bored into him. 'Who you calling kid?'

'No-no offence, mister. I . . . I just thought you and her were getting a mite friendly.' The words faded out as the barkeep felt a knot of fear closing up his throat.

'Shaddup and do what Jabez tells you.'

The way-station keeper tried to call out to his wife, but found his vocal cords had seized up. With blanched features he turned and stumbled to the kitchen door. He gestured feebly to someone inside. 'The stage . . . the stage . . . ' was all he managed in a voice hoarse with fear.

One by one the men drifted outside to await the stage-coach. The fat owner of the station nervously mopped at his perspiring face and neck and contemplated going out the back and clambering on a horse and riding away from the frightening men who had

56

invaded his place. It never occurred to him to make some attempt to release the lawmen tied up next door. To defy this terrible band of men was nowhere on his scope of possibilities.

'Maybe they take a liking to the women and leave me alone.'

With a shaking hand he poured himself a large measure of his potent homebrew.

Outside in the baking sunshine the sinister band of men placed themselves at vantage points around the yard and waited. There was a movement from the corral and their cold eyes watched the two females lead four horses to the hitching rail by the watering trough and tie them in place. The women stood waiting by the horses nervously watching the strange men.

Slowly the stage came into view. No one moved. The men in the yard might have been a group of passengers waiting for the stage.

★　★　★

'Ooooh my aching head.'

Butch Shilton was lying on the earthen floor afraid to move in case the spinning in his head grew worse. For a few idle moments he tried to remember why he had gotten so drunk. For the life of him he could not recall why it was he was lying on the floor, in the dark, nursing the mother of all hangovers.

He could sense movement nearby and was tempted to raise his head and look in that direction, then decided his head might hurt more with movement. Instead, he lay motionless and tried to quell the queasy feeling in his stomach.

Gradually his returning senses detected a steady scraping and a tinny rattling. The activity had a continuous rhythm to it and he thought about what it might be. Then he knew what the noise was.

'Goddamn rats.'

He had vague remembrances of small hairy creatures clambering over him as he lay in the dark and drank himself into oblivion. He had even talked to them and they had talked back. Suddenly he wanted to scratch.

He raised his hand and was puzzled to find his other hand followed involuntarily. For a brief moment he contemplated this strange phenomenon. There was the clink of metal on metal as he brought his hands close to his face and tried to fathom what were the things on his wrists.

'Goddamn manacles.'

Memory came flooding back and he sat up.

Immediately he wished he had followed his first instinct and stayed where he was. His insides heaved and then he was puking up his guts — however, nothing but a vile-tasting liquid was coming up.

'Oh God,' he moaned, 'I wish I were dead.'

'Hi Butch, how you doing?'

'Joe, where the hell are you?'

When the cowboy looked towards the voice he could see a faint rectangle of light from above. The morning sun was shining and finding the cracks in the shuttering that kept them secure.

Moaning softly, he crawled on all fours towards the faint light. He could see the dark hump of someone crouched beneath the outlined rectangle. Before he reached Joe he encountered a soft mound of what seemed like piled up dirt.

'Joe, no sign of that dang blasted Sheriff Patterson yet?'

'Not yet. I hope he stays away a while longer.'

'What you talking about?'

'Butch, while you been lying there in drunken slumber I been digging.'

'Digging!'

'Sure, I took one of them jugs that were lying around and I been digging at this here doorframe. It's only set into the dirt. I reckon if I dug enough the whole thing could be loosened enough to push out.'

Butch stopped crawling and rested. A sweat had broken out and he felt the sickness rise in him again. After he had stopped retching he wiped at his face.

'Damn me, Joe, I feel this is a right fitting place for me right now.'

'How's that?'

'I reckon it couldn't be much worse if I'd died and this was my grave. What time you reckon it is?'

'It's early yet. I heard horses arrive a while back. Thought at first it was the stagecoach, but I think it was just a bunch of riders stopping by for breakfast.'

'Oooh,' Butch moaned, 'breakfast — what the hell's that? Surely the sheriff is bound to feed us today.'

His stomach rumbled, sounding loud in the silent darkness. He rubbed his hand across that suffering organ.

'Mind you, the way I feel I reckon nothing will stay down. I guess I got something fatal.'

'There ain't nothing wrong with you 'cepting you ain't eaten anything in three days. Then you drank ten gallons of rotgut on top of an empty stomach. No wonder you feel bad.'

'Bad! Joe, if you had a gun I'd ask you to put me outta my misery.'

Even as he said this they heard the shots. The sounds were muffled but distinctive. The two fugitives raised their eyes towards the faint rectangle of light that marked the doors of their prison.

'Gunfire,' Butch breathed. 'What the hell's going on out there?'

8

The stagecoach slowed as it came in sight of the way station. With practised ease the driver worked the team of horses, gradually slowing as they approached the station yard. On the seat beside him, riding shotgun, was a large fat man. Up ahead there were men standing around the yard waiting for the arrival of the stagecoach. The driver and his guard thought there was nothing unusual in that.

As the heavy coach wheeled to a halt outside the main building the driver noted the women standing at the corral with the new team. With grunted effort the driver pulled on the brake and sat back in his seat with a sigh. He had been driving all night and was looking forward to a break before taking the stage to Brimingdam where he would be relieved.

The men in the yard watched indolently as the driver climbed down and opened the door of the coach. His shotgun guard took his time clambering down from his perch. Though he was big it was mostly fat and he moved slowly and ponderously as he vacated the coach. He left his shotgun on the seat. Sagging from his waist was a holstered pistol.

'Empire Fastness Way Station,' the driver called out as he unfolded the step. 'Stop here for a whiles. You kin freshen up and git a bite to eat afore we move on.'

He turned and nodded across to the two women holding the replacement horses. For some reason they made no move to bring the fresh team.

''Dadblamed women,' the driver swore. 'Cussed, ornery, dadblamed women.'

He turned back to the coach. A young woman was in the doorway. She looked pale and dusty but managed a wan smile.

'Ma'am,' the driver greeted her. He held out a hand and helped her down. 'Straight over to that door, ma'am. Fat fella inside will look to you.'

Nodding her thanks she waited and an older man in a business suit stepped down. She took his arm and together they walked across and went inside. The gaunt old man nodded and Dave grinned, showing startlingly white teeth and followed the couple inside.

Another man alighted. That he was a drummer was evident from his dress and the sample case he carried. He hurried across the yard. A matronly woman and a young girl emerged followed by a young man dressed in working clothes. As the last of his passengers disappeared inside the way station, the driver, cursing under his breath, turned towards the women with his replacement team.

'Tom, go and see what the hell's the matter with them dadblamed women.'

The guard grunted. He wanted to get inside and fill his belly with whatever eatables were to be had. He started to walk towards the corral, but did not get far.

'Howdy, fella.'

The guard looked at the old man who had stopped him. 'Yeah?'

'What you hauling aboard that there stagecoach?'

The guard's eyes became wary as he eyed the stranger. He felt a slight shiver of fear as he stared into that cold face with the cruel eyes. 'Oh, nothing much, just the mail and a few packages for Brimingdam.'

Another man drifted past him towards the coach. The guard noted two more men standing by the door of the way station.

'Let's just take a look see.'

'Hang on there, mister. That ain't none of your business.'

The guard felt something pressing into his stomach. With a startled look he glanced down at the Colt in the old man's hand. They were standing very close now and the barrel of the gun was

66

pushing hard into the surplus fat of his waist.

'Just walk back to the stage, Fat Boy. Your guts'll explode all over this yard if I havta pull this trigger.'

The driver gulped and went pale. He backed away and kept on reversing.

'Charlie, jump up there and throw down anything you find. You two stand against the stage and don't make a move.'

While the driver and the guard did as they were told, the youngster clambered up on the stage and tossed packages, bundles, trunks and boxes down on the hard-packed earth of the yard.

'That's it, Jabez.'

'OK, let's see what we got?'

The gaunt old man waggled his pistol at the men against the side of the stage. 'Which is the banker's luggage?'

'Banker?' The driver attempted to look puzzled. 'I don't know what you mean.'

The shot hit him in the shoulder. He cried out and fell against the door of the coach. Blood was seeping on to his sleeve.

'The banker's luggage?'

The gun moved to cover the guard. With a trembling hand the fat man pointed at two leather-bound trunks.

'It's those trunks.'

'OK, get them open.'

'Mister, I ain't supposed to tamper with luggage.'

This time the shot hammered into the other shoulder of the driver.

'Oh, my God,' he screamed, and slid to his knees.

The guard hurriedly bent over the trunks and began to undo the straps. 'It's locked,' he said, as he tried to undo the lid.

The guard jumped as shot hammered into the lock. He was sweating from his exertions but mostly from fear.

'Tip it out.'

Grunting with the effort the guard overturned the trunk. Neatly folded shirts and underwear tumbled to the dirt. The last to be exposed were two tin moneyboxes.

'That looks like it, Jabez.'

The youngster who had emptied the coach was back on the ground again.

'Bust it open, Charlie. Use your knife.'

Charlie took a long blade from his belt and knelt by the boxes. With deft movements he prised open the lock. Grinning widely he picked up a neat bundle of notes held together by a paper band. He held up the box so his companion could see inside. It was full to the top with similar bundles of money.

'Look's like your information was correct, Jabez.'

The gun barrel moved fractionally.

'Goodbye, Fat Boy.'

The startled eyes looked up just before the gaunt man pulled the trigger. 'No . . . ' the guard managed, before the bullet ploughed into his stomach.

He staggered back and slammed against the coach, his weight making the coach sway slightly. His hands clasped against his blood-soaked midriff, he slid slowly to the dirt to sit beside the wounded driver.

'You shot me, you goddamn owlhoot.' The guard stared down at the blood leaking through his fingers. 'Damn you to hell.'

'Shall I finish him?' Charlie looked quizzically at his leader. He had his knife in his hand.

'They ain't going nowheres. Let's see what else we got.'

'Marcus.' Jabez turned to one of the men by the door. 'Come and help Charlie search the rest of this. Get those Injun women to load anything of use on the horses.'

Marcus sauntered over and, ignoring the groaning of the two wounded men, he and Charlie began to rummage through the rest of the baggage.

'Let's go inside and see to our guests. Marcus and Charlie can join us when they finished here. Don't forget to bring those Injuns to join us. I think Charlie has taken a shine to the young'un.'

9

'What the hell's that?'

The diggers paused in their labour and strained to listen. Joe felt a shudder run down his spine as he tried to make sense of the shrill noises. Butch pushed higher and put his ear to the thick boards that made up the flaps of the root cellar door.

'If I'm not mistaken that sounds like someone screaming,' he said eventually, a slight tremor in his voice.

The screams grew in intensity. They came in short bursts — high pitched and seemingly unending as of someone in mortal agony.

'Dear God, what the hell's going on up there?'

The men crouched in the darkness and felt the terror invading their prison. Butch put his hands over his ears but nothing could block out those terrible piercing screams.

'Jesus, Joe, this is too scary.'

Butch was whispering. It was insane, for they were buried inside a root cellar some distance from the dreadful agonizing shrieks. However it was an instinctive fear-driven instinct to whisper in the presence of such appalling suffering.

'I've never heard anything like that in my life.'

The big man crouched beside Butch also spoke quietly, his voice trembling as they listened to the dreadful sound of someone in mortal agony. If anything the screaming grew higher in pitch then ceased for a while. The trapped men realized they had been holding their breath and in the relative silence they tried to breathe normally again. It was a short respite. The terrible screams started up again.

'Damnit, stop it!' Butch suddenly yelled. He began hammering on the cellar doors. 'Stop it!'

Joe grabbed his companion and

dragged him back. 'Goddamn it, Butch, don't attract their attention,' he panted, as he wrestled with his fellow prisoner. 'It's probably a bunch of Injuns as has overrun the place. They're scalping and torturing their victims right now.'

'We gotta help them,' Butch panted.

'How, goddamn it, how?' Joe said bitterly. 'We're trapped in here. We're handcuffed and with no weapons. What the hell can we do against a bunch of armed savages?'

'We oughta do something,' the cowboy answered distractedly, as the terrible screams battered at their sanity. 'I can't stand it.'

'Butch, we gotta sit this one out. If they don't know we're here maybe we'll survive. Sheriff Patterson mighta got himself killed during the attack. If he has then no one else will bother with us. Remember there was only a brief spell of shooting. They musta overrun the place very quickly. We attract attention to ourselves they'll come and drag us out and roast our innards over a slow fire, or whatever Injuns do to their prisoners.'

'Hell, I need a drink.'

Butch stumbled back to the vats where he had indulged last night. After a few moments Joe went back and joined him. Butch had been using a discarded tin mug to dip in the potent liquor. Joe could just make out his tilted head as he slugged back the contents of the mug. Without a word Butch refilled the mug and handed it to Joe. The big man coughed as the fiery liquor hit the back of his throat but forced the rest down.

The screaming went on for a very long time. By the time it ceased altogether the prisoners were at first not aware of it. They were barely conscious as they forced mug after mug of firewater inside them in an attempt to drown out the terror and fear both felt. It somewhat dulled the edges of their imagination as the screams of the victims penetrated their dim, clammy prison. They knew dark and appalling deeds were being committed yards from where they huddled together in the pit.

The liquor was an antidote to their feeling of helplessness. In a curious twist of conscience they felt guilty of conspiracy with the perpetrators of the evil acts of depravity being committed up there in the way station.

'Butch, you awake?'

'Humph . . . '

'It's stopped.'

There was silence as they listened. A heavy and curious silence lay over everything like a shroud. Groaning with the effort of overcoming the sluggishness induced by the numerous mugs of rotgut they had consumed they crawled underneath the trapdoor that had so stubbornly resisted their labours. Lethargically they resumed their digging.

Their handcuffs did not impede their working. Both hands were able to hold the digging tool and though the metal chaffed their wrists it did not bother them too much. After a long spell of effort Butch finally spoke.

'Joe, I got something to tell you.'

'Yeah, you decided to swear off drink.'

'Mmmm . . . maybe, but something else.'

There was another long pause.

'You know last night when I was drinking all that rotgut?'

'You fell into a drunken sleep and pissed your pants.'

Butch was silent so long Joe ceased his efforts and glanced at him. He could just see a dim outline as the cowboy dug at the side of the cellar with a large paddle he had found in one of the barrels.

'I guessed right then, you did piss your pants?'

'Not exactly.'

Joe suddenly started giggling. 'You messed your pants.'

'Goddamn it, no! It's to do with piss though. You see, I was bursting to go. My bladder was full to overflowing.' Joe could hear the cowboy take a deep breath before continuing. 'So I went in one of the barrels.'

Joe stopped digging. 'For Gawd's sake, you pissed in a barrel? Did it have anything in?'

'They all have.'

Joe thought about this for a moment. 'Before we leave here we oughta tip it out.'

'The thing is, Joe I don't think we can.'

'Why ever not? It'll just soak into the dirt. It wouldn't be fair to leave for someone to drink rotgut what has been flavoured with Butch Shilton piss. Mind you, that stuff is so vile it would be hard to tell the difference.'

'The fact of the matter is, I can't remember which barrel.'

Joe ceased digging. Butch stopped also.

'You can't remember which barrel?' Joe asked, in a dangerously quiet voice.

'Hell, Joe, I was drunk outta my skin. I didn't know where I was, never mind what barrel.'

Joe was quiet for so long the cowboy was moved to speak. 'Joe, you OK?'

'So there was every chance when I joined you back there for a drink I might have been drinking your piss?'

'Hell should I know!'

'Aaagh . . . '

The sound of furious spitting was heard. Butch listened apprehensively.

'Butch Shilton, remind me when we get outta here to kill you.'

There was a sudden scramble in the dark. Butch, thinking his companion was attacking him, threw himself backwards and flailed wildly with his paddle. An abrupt flash of white light blinded him as brilliant sunlight flooded the root cellar. He caught sight of Joe sitting by the trapdoor half buried in dirt. The big man turned his head and Butch saw a flash of white teeth in a dirt-encrusted face.

'Butch, did you ever see a more wonderful sight? God's good clean sunlight.'

10

Like prairie dogs warily coming to the surface they raised their heads above ground level blinking in the bright daylight. There was not much to see from this side of the way station. On the right was the corral where a few horses moved restlessly. They peered around them cautiously, ready to duck back again at any sign of danger. An ominous silence lay over everything.

'Seems mighty quiet.'

'Too quiet for my liking.'

Covered in dirt that adhered to faces and clothing, they clambered to freedom. Both men stretched luxuriously, pushing their handcuffed hands above their heads.

'It's good to get the kinks outta my body.'

'It'd be even better to get some grub inside me. My insides feel like they been scoured out with a grass rake.'

Keeping close against the wall of the building they edged forward and peered round the corner. The first thing they noticed was the coach. Movement by the wheels drew their eyes. Both men peered with some bewilderment at the huge birds tearing at the wheels of the coach.

'What the . . . ?'

Slowly they moved from the protection of the building and out into the yard. All around were scattered garments and valises and trunks. Men's shirts and trousers and women's dresses and blouses and undergarments littered the earth. They could make out what seemed like red and white rags attached to the wheels of the stage. It was these the birds were busy tearing at. Disturbed by the movement of the men the vultures wheeled around and screeched aggressively.

'Oh my God.'

The tattered carcasses were the remains of two men. They had been lashed to the wheels while still alive and left for the vultures.

'Shoo, get away, you bloody vultures!'

Butch and Joe stumbled forward waving their arms and shouting. For a moment it looked as if the birds might defy them but at the last moment they took flight — their broad wings lifting heavy bodies laboriously into the air.

Their eyes filled with horror, the two men stared at the pitiful remains of the driver and his guard. Sickened by the awful sight of ripped flesh they turned and looked around the yard at the scattered remnants of luggage.

'Looks like we're the only ones left. Let's see what we can find inside. We need grub and some way of getting free of these damned handcuffs.'

'What the hell's that smell?'

They both stood in the yard sniffing the strange sickly odour that seemed to cling to their nostrils.

'I smelled that afore when we butchered a steer on the ranch,' answered Butch. 'Must be them two poor fellas the buzzards were at.'

'Let's see what we can find inside.'

They stepped inside then abruptly both men tumbled outdoors again. They flattened against the outside wall — one each side of the door.

'Joe.'

'Butch.'

'Tell me I'm still down that root cellar and I'm drunk outta my skull and my brain is unhinged with alcohol. Tell me I didn't see what I thought I saw in there.'

Joe did not answer for some time. Both men were trembling and their breathing was rapid and agitated.

'Gawddamn it, Butch, you were sure right about that butchered steer. You got the smell right but the wrong animal. What we gonna do?'

Joe was turning his head from side to side like a trapped animal looking for an escape route.

'There's some horses out the corral. I say we get on them and ride.'

'Where'll we go?'

'I don't know. I guess anywhere will do as long as it's away from this hellhole.'

'Butch, we can't just ride away. What about those people . . . those bodies inside?'

'Hell, what can we do for them. It's a slaughterhouse in there.'

'You see the blood? It's like it were painted on the floors and walls.'

'Don't, Joe, don't say anything about it. I think I'm gonna be sick again.'

They were silent for a while trying not to think too much of the horror they had just glimpsed inside the way station.

'Butch, did you notice if Sheriff Patterson was among that there . . . I mean . . . oh Gawd . . . if Sheriff Patterson's dead that means we're kinda free.'

'Yeah, sorta, but if we ride around wearing these cuffs we'll be picked up sooner or later. We oughta go round the back and find something to cut ourselves free.'

They almost ran around the back of the station. The dilapidated outhouses yielded up nothing they could use on the cuffs. Uneasily they approached the rear door of the station and stood outside.

'These are the back rooms. There'll be stores or kitchens or something.'

At first they only noticed the rows of bunks. Silently they moved inside. Then they saw Sheriff Patterson and his deputy, Uncle John. Once more they had to look on a scene of horror.

'He was a bastard but he didn't deserve that.'

The lawmen had been suspended from a beam. Someone with a bizarre sense of the macabre had fashioned proper hanging nooses. Their blackened faces and protruding tongues were some indication that they had died from strangulation rather than broken necks. They stared with sick fascination at the gruesome sight.

'Joe, there's something mighty strange about all this. We assuming it were Injuns as did all this? No Injun would hang a fella like that. No Injun would go to the bother to make a noose just to hang someone.'

'White men?'

'Renegades.' The cowboy pointed towards the doorway leading to the front. 'The butchery inside — them fellas outside tied to the stage. And now this.' He shook his head. 'It weren't no Injun did this. I reckon a gang of renegades came through here.' His eyes widened as a thought struck him. 'You realize we're alive because we were locked in that there cellar. Them fellas didn't know about us otherwise you and I woulda been butchered too.'

'Let's cut them down. It don't seem right to leave them hanging like that.'

While searching for a blade they found Sheriff Patterson's gunbelt lying underneath a bunk. His twin Remingtons were still in the holster but there was no knife.

'Look in his pocket.'

They found a clasp knife and during

the search a bunch of keys.

'Gawddamn it, Joe. It looks as if we're free of these handcuffs without having to file them off.'

Respectfully they laid the two bodies on the bunks and covered them with blankets.

'You think we should do the same for the folk out there?'

'Let's find something to eat first. The kitchen should be around here somewheres.'

The got the stove going and started a pot boiling for coffee. There was a store of dried beans and they put them in a pan with water. Adding mouldy potatoes they boiled up a mess. The stew along with some stale bread made an unappetizing but satisfying meal. This activity had kept them from thinking too much about the butchery that had gone on around them.

'Butch, I been thinking. I remember reading once about a Viking funeral.'

'Yeah, what about it?' the stocky cowboy replied indistinctly, through a mouthful of half-chewed bread.

'These Vikings would put the fella as had died on board his favourite ship and set the whole thing damn alight.'

For a moment Butch stopped chewing. 'Gawdamn it, Joe, we could do it, too. There must be kerosene around here somewheres and we can get straw from the stables.' He paused for a moment, a frown creasing his dirt-encrusted face. 'Would we havta go inside?'

'One of us oughta go in to make sure the place is gonna burn properly. Just slosh the kerosene about.'

They sat in silence as they contemplated the terrible sights they had witnessed inside the main room of the way station. Neither wanted to be the one to go inside.

'We could draw straws.'

'The screaming, Joe — that woulda been the folk inside there.'

'I guess. Sheriff Patterson and Uncle John surely wouldn't have been able to scream. Not with a rope round their necks.'

'What makes men do things like that, you reckon?'

'I dunno, Butch. Sure beats all reason.' Joe sighed deeply. 'Let's get started. The sooner I'm away from this hellish abattoir the better.'

11

Before they started on their ghoulish task of cremating the dead in Empire Fastness Way Station the escapees saddled two of the horses in the corral. They scavenged as much food as was portable and used a third horse as a pack animal.

Though feeling rather queasy about wearing a dead man's rig Butch strapped on the sheriff's twin Remington pistols while Joe did the same with Uncle John's Colt. While rummaging in the coach Joe came across the guard's shotgun and two boxes of shells which he added to their arsenal.

In the clear blue sky above them, as they worked at their tasks, the vultures soared in the hot air currents and waited for the activity at the way station to cease. They had tasted the flesh of the dead and hungered for more.

'What about those fellas tied to the coach?'

They eyed the grisly remains of the driver and his guard and the stodgy food in their bellies shifted uneasily.

'Couldn't we just set the coach on fire?'

'I don't reckon so. The coach will just burn around them. I guess they'll be better off inside.'

In the end they draped blankets over the shredded corpses. It made it only slightly easier to cut away the bonds that held them to the wheels. Quickly rolling the bodies in the blankets they carried them separately across the littered yard to the door of the main building. Sweat was pouring freely down their faces by the time they finished placing the bundles.

'We havta take them inside.'

'Hell, Joe, we both gotta do this,' Butch said desperately. 'We get the kerosene and the straw and then we both rush in and set it.'

'What the hell's that?'

Drifting in from the prairie and into the yard the voice of the singer arrived at the Way Station before he did.

'It was Big Nose Kate that done me down.
I met her in Barwell town.
She took my gold and she took my life
I guess I wanted her for my wife.'

The singer broke off as he stared at the two villainous men confronting him. One pointed a pistol while the other trained a shotgun at him.

'My, it looks as if I've fallen amongst desperate men.'

He was an aged fellow with mahogany skin and eyes an alert, deep brown. He stared unafraid at the desperadoes confronting him. Shifting a big wad to his other cheek he spat then went back to regarding the two saddle bums.

They were hatless and their faces and clothes were smeared with dirt. Neither of the pair had shaved for days. There was desperation in their eyes and he saw the gaunt and hollow look on their faces of men pushed to the extremes of endurance.

'What you doing here, mister?' the bigger of the two asked.

The old man spat again — a long stringy brown spit before replying. 'I was coming in for supplies.' He gestured to the packhorse he was trailing.

The two men glanced uncertainly at each other. Waiting patiently on top his horse the old-timer spat again as he took in the destruction of the luggage in the yard.

'Looks like there's been a mite of trouble here.'

The men regarded him steadily.

'I don't think he's one of them, Joe.'

'One of who, young fella?'

Joe gestured around the yard with his shotgun. 'The fellas as did this.'

'I saw a bunch of mean-looking fellas riding hard back a piece.' He eyed his captors speculatively. 'You ain't part of that gang, are you?'

'Hell, no, old-timer. We was . . . ' Joe hesitated. 'We just arrived ourselves. We was figuring on . . . hell, we was gonna set fire to the place and let these poor people rest in peace.'

Ignoring the weapons pointed at him, the newcomer dismounted. 'I could do with a drink. Let's go inside. You fellas can tell me all about it.'

'I wouldn't go inside, old man. It's a butcher's shop in there.'

'That bad, eh? You mind if I have a peek?'

Joe and Butch followed the man across the littered yard. After regarding the blanket-covered forms resting outside the door the stranger stepped inside. The two friends waited. It was a while before the old man reappeared. His mahogany skin was a shade paler than when he first went in.

'There's a fella still alive in there.'

★ ★ ★

Joe and Butch busted out a bunk and carried it inside trying not to look too much at the carnage. They found the old man kneeling by the side of a young man. His stomach had been opened and his intestines spilled out on the floor. Gagging on their recently consumed meal the two lifted him on to the makeshift stretcher.

'What about . . . ?'

Butch was pointing with horrified eyes at the blood-encrusted entrails that had been dragged from the youngster. For answer the old-timer gathered up what seemed like yards of intestine and piled it on the bunk beside the dying man. They carried their gruesome burden from the room, averting their eyes from impaled bodies on tables — some flayed, some hacked about.

Helplessly they stood about and looked anywhere but at the man they had carried into the sleeping quarters.

'Ain't there anything we can do?' Joe turned pleading eyes to the old man.

The old man shook his head. 'A sip

of water — bathe his face. He's dying. It's just a matter of when.' He spat on to the floor. 'I seen some bad things in my seventy years but that stuff in there — that's the stuff of nightmares. If someone tells me the end of the world is just around the corner I reckon I'll believe him.' He wiped at his lips. 'I could do with a drink. You fellas know where there's any? I don't feel like going back in that bar again.'

'Yeah, there's a cellar full of the stuff. I'll fetch some up. We all could do with a drink.'

Joe disappeared out the back. As he left on his errand there was a low groan from the dying man. Butch stared with horrified expression at the butchered body on the bunk. The cowboy bent closer to the grey face. Suddenly the eyes snapped open.

'Edie!'

'Take it easy, fella. The sawbones is on his way. We'll look after you till he arrives.'

'Edie . . . my sister . . . they took

Edie. She's only a kid.'

A hand reached up and gripped Butch by the shirt. For a dying man the grip was surprisingly strong. The cowboy stared helplessly, unable to move.

'Get her back for me, you hear.' The voice was urgent.

'Sure . . . fella . . . sure . . . I'll get her back.'

'Promise me!'

Butch made no reply, not knowing what to do. Beside him he heard the old man spit.

'Promise . . . ' The eyes were wild and staring. 'Promise me you'll save her from those savages. Promise!' With the last vestiges of his dying strength the man held Butch rigidly before him. 'Promise . . . I won't go till you promise. Promise you'll get my sister back.'

'I promise . . . I'll get her back . . . I promise.'

Butch was still crouched over the body when Joe appeared carrying a couple of jugs. The old man reached out and prised the dead man's hand from Butch's shirt.

'He's dead, fella. It's a blessin' he's gone.'

There were tears in the cowboy's eyes when he looked up. 'Why, old-timer? Why butcher people like that?'

The old man turned and walked over to Joe and took a jug from him. He put it to his head and began to drink. Joe walked across to Butch.

'What happened?'

Butch took the other jug from him and took a long swig before replying. 'He's dead. Afore he died he asked me to go after his sister.' There were tears streaming down Butch's face as he stared back at his friend. 'Joe, he made me promise. He made me promise to get back his sister.'

12

They sat their horses and watched the smoke spew up into the clear skies. The dark plume rose up like a cloud of sinister insects swarming into the heavens. No one spoke for a while. They just sat there watching — drained of all emotion. The only sound from time to time was of the old-timer spitting.

Before they left the way station they had learned a little bit about the man. His name was Frank McCrae and he drifted around doing a little trapping and prospecting. He was an occasional visitor at Empire Fastness, stopping off to stock up on liquor and supplies.

Butch sighed deeply. He was the first one to speak. 'I guess this is where we part.'

Joe pushed his hat to the back of his head and scratched at his forehead.

'You set on following those killers?'

'I promised. I guess a promise to a dying man is binding.'

'Well, I got nowhere in particular to go. I might just tag along for a piece.'

The cowboy's brow cleared slightly. 'I sure would be grateful for any help.'

'Hang on there. I didn't say I would help. I said as I would tag along for a piece, is all.'

Beside them Frank spat. 'You know what direction they took?' he asked.

'I guess I'll cast around for a spell see if I can pick up their trail.'

'I saw them hightailin' it yonder.' The old man pointed. 'I counted ten or so hosses. Some would have been pack-horses and if'n they was takin' females as captives that would make mebbe seven fighters. A lot of killers for two fellas to take on.'

'I ain't said as I was going after those killers,' Joe protested. 'I just said as I would tag along for a piece.'

Butch swung his horse around in the direction the old man had indicated.

'So long, old-timer. Thanks for all your help back there.'

'I didn't do much.' Spit. 'Come to think on it, mebby I bin alone too long. I guess I'll ride a'ways with you fellas.'

They camped that night in a dry arroyo. There wasn't much talk. Each was sunk in his own thoughts. The terrible sights they had witnessed back at the Empire Fastness Way Station weighed heavily on them all.

Frank took out a harmonica and drew forth a haunting tune that left them all feeling nostalgic for better times.

'How you gonna know them fellas?' Joe asked at last. 'We none of us saw them. Frank only saw them from afar.'

'I guess I'll just follow their tracks. When I meet up with a bunch of fellas as is trailing along a young woman that'll be them.'

'When you meet up! When you meet up then you'll be dead. Them fellas are killers. I don't need to remind you what they done back at that way station.

They meant to leave no witnesses. They killed everyone — the people at the way station, the passengers on the stage, and Sheriff Patterson and Uncle John. Everyone!'

After spitting into the fire, Frank eyed the two youngsters. 'How come you know this sheriff and Uncle John? They friends of yourn?'

There was an uneasy silence as the men considered the question.

'Hell, Frank, you might as well know. The sheriff was escorting us to the penitentiary. Judge Pleasance, back in Hinkly, sentenced Butch here to ten years for pleasuring his young wife. I got ten for killing a tinhorn cardsharp. I figure it was 'cause the judge was still mad at Butch I got such a heavy sentence. The sheriff penned us in the root cellar while he and his deputy spent the night comfortable in those bunks. I guess in a way Sheriff Patterson saved our lives putting us in that cellar.'

'Ten years seems a mite harsh for

killin' a cardsharp. As for pleasurin' the judge's wife, that is serious.'

'How the hell you make that out, old-timer? The way I figure it it's not so serious as killing someone.'

'I don't rightly know the details of the killin' but if'n he was a card sharp as Joe killed, then I guess he musta caught him cheatin'. Could be rightly what they calls justifiable homicide. You'da thought the judge would'a taken that into consideration. But to covet another man's wife.' The old man shook his head. 'You deserved all you got.'

'Ah hell, you dried-up old fart, you don't know what you're on about. If the woman's willing and the husband don't find out then what's the harm? And anyhow the judge didn't catch me out. He just found me in his garden with no clothes on and he put two and two together.'

'Hell, Butch, you never told me that part of it. You was prancing around the judge's garden naked?' Suddenly Joe started chortling. 'Naked! Well if that don't beat all. I never heard of no naked gardener afore.'

'Gawddamn it, Joe,' the cowboy was becoming irritated. 'I weren't gardening; I was trying to get away from the judge.'

The big man's shoulders were shaking as he tried to stifle his merriment. 'I hope you weren't pruning no holly bushes. That could be a mite tricky. And don't suppose you could do much with the prickly pear. You would have set yourself a thorny problem there.'

'Aw, go to hell!'

The cowboy picked up a piece of firewood and shied it across at his giggling companion. Joe fell back and howled. He couldn't contain his laughter. 'Gawdamn naked . . . ' And he was off again.

It was too much. Butch launched himself across at the giggling man and began pummelling him. Joe was laughing so much he could not defend himself.

'Naked!' he gasped. 'Judge Pleasance

caught you naked in his garden. Was her name Eve? Did she offer you an apple?' And he was off again.

'Damn you, her name was Eleanor, not Eve!'

But the annoyance Butch felt was melting under the mirth of his helpless companion. Suddenly he cottoned on to the connection Joe was making between the apple the garden and Eve.

'Damn you, you're an ungodly maggot, Joe Peters.'

He could feel Joe shaking beneath him, still convulsed with mirth. In the end Butch rolled from atop his gleeful companion. Listening to Joe's guffaws, in spite of himself, the cowboy couldn't help smiling as he stared up at the starlit sky. They had been acquainted for only a few days and those days were marred by bloody events back at the way station. But he was already growing fond of the irrepressible carpenter.

'Joe, I sure wish you'd change your mind about accompanying me.'

Joe sat up wiping at his eyes.

'You know, Butch, I can't remember the last time I laughed like that. Changes a man's perspective. Maybe I just will go along. Come to think on it, I ain't got nowhere else to go right now.'

13

'How far you reckon they're ahead?' Joe asked.

By now they had got used to the old-timer spitting to emphasize each sentence he uttered. They had found the remains of a camp and Frank had examined the site declaring it was almost certain the raiders had stopped overnight.

'I figger two days at least. They're headin' somewheres safe to hole up is what I reckon. They're gonna lie low till the next killin'. Which makes me wonder if'n they were after somethin' specific on that there stage. Mebby gold bullion or somethin' the like.'

'You could be right, Frank. Those *hombres* made sure there was no witnesses. Only we were there no one woulda found those bodies till the next stage was due, or someone like you came along. By which time they're long gone. And if nobody saw them no one can pin the killings on them.'

'Beats me why they took the girl with them,' Butch interjected. 'Surely she's a witness?'

'They don't intend fer her to live, young fella. My guess they've taken her along fer sport. When they tire of her she'll end up like the others back at Empire Fastness Way Station with her throat slit.'

'Gawddamn it, Frankie, do you have to be so specific?'

'I'da thought it was obvious after what you seen back there.'

'Yeah, well, you don't need to spell it out for me.'

Frank moved his wad about his mouth and spat over his horse's head. 'Fer a hardened jailbird you seem a mite naive. Them fellas is killers and right brutal ones at that. They ain't satisfied at straightforward murder, but they get a satisfaction from inflictin' pain. You fellas told me the screams of their victims went on fer some time. Takes a special kinda killer to inflict so much sufferin'.'

'Damnit, Frank, I ain't no hardened criminal. It was just a set of unfortunate circumstances that got me a prison sentence. You can't compare me with those murdering sonsofbitches. I promised that fella as I would try and get back his sister from them renegades. It don't make me feel any better for you to tell me she'll be more'n likely dead afore I find her.'

'OK, OK, keep your hair on. I'm only statin' facts. Anyways we oughta find water soon. Them hosses'll need waterin'. That feed you brung from Empire Fastness will keep them goin' for a while yet, but we need to find water for them.'

'Well, I reckon we oughta come across a creek sometime. If not, we'll havta be on the lookout for a ranch house and get our water there.'

It was well past noon when they sighted the building. They had been thinking of stopping for a meal break and were looking for a suitable place to rest up.

'Now that's a welcome sight.' Butch observed. 'We'll mosey on down there and use their watering place. Maybe invite us in for a meal. I don't reckon I've had a decent meal in weeks. Just think on it — home cooking. Fresh bread just off the pan. Real coffee with molasses stirred in. My juices is running already.'

'Butch, you really take the biscuit. Ever since I met you all you ever think about is food.'

The cowboy grinned at his companion. 'When a man has a full belly and a plump woman in bed with him he's halfways to paradise. Don't you ever yearn to be back East snuggled up with that little wife of yours rather than riding the owlhoot tail with a couple of rogues?'

'I ain't no rogue,' objected Frank. 'I'm a respectable drifter. Never run foul of the law. Well, only once or twice fer drunk and disorderly.'

The shot came from the house and whipped past the old-timer as he spoke. 'Hell damnit!'

Another shot whistled near and they pulled the horses around and raced for a strand of stunted trees.

'Hey, what the hell you firing at us for?' Butch yelled once they dismounted. 'We don't mean no harm. We come friendly.'

The reply was another shot that whizzed harmlessly overhead. They crouched low among the trees out of sight of the marksman.

'We was figuring on watering our horses,' Butch yelled again. 'What the hell's happened to Western hospitality?'

They cringed expecting another shot but this time the shooter shouted back to them. 'There's a creek two mile further on. Just look for the line of cottonwoods.'

'All right, gawddamn it, we're going. But no more shooting.'

'As long as you keep moving I ain't

shooting. If you plan on pulling any tricks the next shots will be a mite lower.'

'Joe, I reckon that voice is female. You think she's all alone in there?'

'Butch, it matters little if she's alone or not. She's got a gun trained on us. Let's just mosey on down to that creek she's told us about. We can water our horses without getting full of holes.'

'Yeah, I wonder how purty she is.'

'Damn me if you ain't the limit, Butch. She's probably an old biddy with warts and a hairy chin. More'n likely she smells of piss and would as soon put a spell on us as shoot us. Now we don't want any more trouble. We got enough piling up ahead when we catch up with them there renegades.'

Cautiously they began to lead their horses out from the bushes.

'Don't shoot!' Butch yelled. 'We're going quietly.' He looked round. 'Now where the hell's Frank got to?'

There was a sudden scream from the house and a shot. Instinctively the pals ducked expecting a bullet coming their way. There was another scream.

'Hell's bells, there's some trouble up at that house,' Butch yelled.

Before Joe could stop him he had leapt on his horse and was galloping towards the ranch buildings.

'Wait, Butch, it might be a trick,' Joe yelled, but the cowboy did not hear. He was rapidly closing up the distance to the ranch.

'Gawddamn you, Butch Shilton,' Joe yelled in frustration. 'He thinks he's Sir Galahad rescuing fair damsels in distress.'

Then he, too, was riding after his companion and cursing as he went.

14

They hit the yard without any more shots being fired. Joe was a few yards behind his cowboy partner. Almost as the horses pulled up, the two men slid from the saddles and flung themselves on to the front porch. They flattened against each side of the door. Both had revolvers in their hands — Butch with one of Sheriff Patterson's Remingtons and Joe with his purloined Colt.

Now they were up close they could see the house was dilapidated and neglected. The porch sagged in the middle and the door had not seen paint for a considerable number of seasons.

Keeping his back against the wall of the house Butch reached out cautiously and tried the latch on the ramshackle front door. It lifted easily. He waited while they both listened. They were puzzled by the apparent silence from the house after the shooting and screaming.

Taking a deep breath Butch pushed hard and the door swung open. He risked a quick peep around the doorpost. Nothing happened. He looked across at Joe and signed to him he was about to enter. Joe readied himself and nodded. The cowboy dived low and rolled inside, his Remington at the ready. When there was no immediate gunfire Joe quickly followed.

'Howdy, fellas, I wondered if'n you were gonna join us.'

'Frank!'

The men stared with some puzzlement at the old-timer. He was sitting on a chair with a rifle held across his knees. As usual he was chewing his baccy. Against the far wall a young woman cowered. She was staring at the newcomers with frightened eyes.

'While you fellas were being shot at I sneaked in round the back and took this rifle off'n this here female. I tried to tell her we meant her no harm but my guess is she's had trouble afore with riders.'

Both Joe and Butch removed their hats and nodded reassuringly at the woman. They holstered their weapons before speaking.

'Ma'am, we spoke true when we said as we just wanted to water our horses. We won't hurt you.'

As they regarded the woman they realized she was only a girl. She was dressed in a ragged shirt and jeans. Her face was streaked with dirt. The tracks of tears were visible on her cheeks where the wetness had eroded some of the grime.

'Where's your folk? Surely you don't live here alone?'

She was trembling as she stood up. Self-consciously she brushed at the strands of dirty blonde hair. She gestured towards the back of the house and walked towards the door. The men looked at each other, shrugged and followed.

Her folk were laid out in the barn.

They had been savagely beaten before they died. An elderly man and what must have been his equally elderly wife. The men stared with some concern at the grisly sight of the two corpses.

'They been through here,' Joe whispered.

They looked with some sympathy at the young girl. Tears were running afresh down her grubby cheeks.

'I'm sorry, miss. No wonder you fired at us. We're following the monsters as done this. They murdered some more folk a piece back in Empire Fastness Way Station. We been trailing them ever since. Would you like for us to bury your folk afore we move on?'

'Yes, please.'

The girl could not hold back her sobs. Joe moved instinctively and put an arm around her.

'Why don't you go back in the house and make us some coffee,' the big man told her. 'When we dug the holes we'll call you.'

It was Frank who lent some dignity

to the burial ceremony. He produced a well-thumbed Bible and read a few passages.

''Where thou diest, will I die, and there will I be buried; the Lord do so to me, and more also, if aught but death part thee and me. And he will make his burial place even with the wicked ones, and with the rich class in his death, despite the fact that he had done no violence and there was no deception in his mouth'.'

As they sat in the house and cooked up a meal they quizzed the girl about her plans. Her name was Jessica Kelsey and she was fifteen years of age. She had been sent up to the top pastures to bring in the milk cows when the raiders rode through. Hearing the commotion she had run back to find out what was happening. Seeing so many horses in the yard she had hung back. Then she had seen her father and mother being dragged outside. The raiders had taken turns beating them with whatever farm implements were at hand. She had hidden till they looted what little wealth there was and ridden away.

'How many were there?'

There were five men and they had two women with them who took no part in the killing of her parents. Neither had they made any protest over their brutal treatment.

'Two women — that fella said nothing about two women. He only mentioned his sister.'

'Can you describe these people to us?'

Her eyes seemed to glaze over. 'I'll never forget them. One older man, thin and bony. Four younger ones. One tall and dark — one short and thick — one slight of build and dark and one about the size of Butch and dark also.'

'What about the women — can you describe them?'

'A very young girl about my age and an older woman. Not old-old but older than the girl. Might have been her mother.'

Joe shook his head. 'Nah, can't be her

mother. Musta been some other poor female taken hostage. Trouble is we don't know who was on the stage or who was at the station. The second woman coulda been from Empire Fastness.'

'Nope,' Frank interrupted. 'The only females at the station was an Injun woman and her halfwit daughter. I saw them both back there, God rest their souls. Looks to me this other woman was a passenger on the stage. I pity them both.'

'Please take me with you when you go.'

The three men looked at each other and then back at the young girl.

'Jessica, you don't know what you're asking. Have you no folk you can go to?'

She shook her head, her large eyes pleading with them. 'No one — there was just my parents and me.'

'We . . . we're three men on the trail of a bunch of killers,' Joe stated. 'We can't take care of no child.'

'I'm no child,' Jessica protested. 'I'm fifteen. And I can shoot too. I always brought home game for the pot.'

'Joe, we can't leave her here,' Butch intervened. 'I say we take her on to the next big town.'

It was Frank who decided the issue. 'Ain't you fellas forgettin' this little gal is the only one as seen them there killers? She can identify them and not only that, if we get them to the law she can testify what they done to her ma an pa.'

15

The city of Coventree was a vast conurbation of clapboard buildings. The little band, now numbering four with the addition of Jessica, rode up the main street and stopped at the livery.

'What we supposed to use for money?' Joe asked, eyeing the livery stable. 'They ain't gonna put up our horses for free.'

'I figger I can grubstake you fellas,' Frank answered, spitting over his horse's head. 'I got a little put by.'

'That's mighty swell of you, Frank,' Butch observed. 'I dunno when we'll be able to repay you.'

'I got some money,' Jessica said, and blushed. Once the men had agreed to take her along she had ridden with them in silence, only speaking when spoken to. 'Ma always had a tin of money she said she was keeping for a rainy day.' She sniffed, suddenly remembering what had happened to her parents. 'I guess she wouldn't mind me lending you some.'

When the liveryman took charge of their mounts they enquired about lodgings. They were directed to a boarding-house.

'I reckon we'll stay at least one night here and make enquiries about them killers,' Butch suggested. 'It looks as if they were heading this way. They may have stopped to replenish supplies. Someone might have seen them. We oughta parcel out the likely places and make the rounds.'

In the end, Butch and Jessica were to make a round of the boarding-houses, eating-houses and hotels. Frank was to mosy round the stores and places of business while Joe took it on himself to look into the saloons and places of entertainment.

'We meet back at the livery in an hour or so and confab,' Joe suggested. 'Whatever happens, no one should confront those fellas. Remember, they're killers.'

He tried three saloons without success, asking if a group of men and two women had stopped by for refreshments. Then he contemplated the sporting houses and wondered if Butch might be better at that sort of enquiry.

His fourth saloon was called the Good Eva Arcadia and seemed much livelier than the previous places he had visited. There was a baccarat table as well as roulette and a couple of card games going. Joe ambled in and ordered a beer.

'Nope,' the barkeep replied to Joe's enquiry regarding the men they were seeking. 'Best ask down at the livery. They see everyone as comes an' goes.'

'Now why didn't I think of that?' Joe observed ruefully.

He wandered among the crowd idly watching the games in progress and sizing up the men in the saloon. No one matched the descriptions Jessica had given. He stopped at one table where four men were playing poker. Fingering the few dollars he had in his pocket he was tempted to sit in but the betting was way beyond his means. He was more hopeful at the next table. There was a pile of dimes in the centre of the table indicating the level of play. Joe asked for a place and was accepted into the low stakes poker school.

* * *

'We ain't sure how long we'll stay,' Frank told the liveryman. 'Can I pay you each day?'

'Sure, old-timer. That'll be two dollars for corral and feed.'

'You ain't seen a bunch of fellas come through here in the last day or two? Mebby five men and a couple of women.'

'Reckon I did, old-timer. Mean-looking bunch of fellas. Came by yesterday. Friends of yourn?'

Frank's alert old eyes lit up at hitting

124

paydirt so soon. 'Yeah, we was supposed to meet up but we missed 'em. Where'll I find 'em?'

'Not in Coventree that's for sure. They lit out soon after buying fresh hosses.'

'Damnit, I seem fated to miss those rannies. Anyone they saw in particular that can throw some light on where they went?'

'That's the strange thing. They all congregated down at Mr Miller's house. Spent some time down there. Not the sorta fellas I would have thought Mr Miller woulda knowed.'

'Oh, and why's that?'

'Mr Miller is the richest man in this town. He owns the Westmoreland Bank. In fact he owns most things in Coventree.'

'Mr Miller owns the bank,' Frank repeated thoughtfully. 'Whereabouts will I find him?'

'His house is a big white building down at the south end of town. Can't miss it. Got them pillars outside.

Regular mansion it is. When he's not down at the bank that's where you'll find him.'

Frank thought his information was so important he decided to seek out his friends and share it with them. He caught up with Butch and Jessica as they stood on a corner debating which direction to take.

'That is as good a place as any to start,' opined the cowboy. 'Let's head down to this Mr Miller.'

The house was very grand with roman-style columns adorning the front and an elaborately decorated porch.

'I guess he must be purty rich to live in a house like this,' Frank ventured. 'It ain't the sorta place I've ever been in.'

'Me neither,' Butch agreed. 'But hell, we gotta ask.'

As they started forward Jessica held back. 'I . . . don't feel right going in a house like that. I only ever lived in that old ranch house with Ma and Pa.'

'Look, Jessica, just 'cause he lives in a high-class house don't mean he's any better than us,' Frank assured her.

But nothing would persuade her to accompany them. 'I'll go back to the boarding-house and wait for you.'

'That liveryman was right when he said it seemed strange those renegades came avisitin' down here.' Frank observed as they walked up the long, tree-lined drive.

'Damn strange.'

A liveried black servant opened the door to their knock. His look of disdain was evident as he took in the bedraggled state of the visitors.

'We're here to see Mr Miller,' Butch said.

Those condescending eyes looked them up and down. It was plain that Mr Miller's servant resented two saddle tramps dirtying up the master's immaculate porch.

'All tradesmen round the back,' he said, and abruptly closed the door.

'Doggone if I would pull that uppity black fella out here and trounce him,' the cowboy spluttered.

He was about to raise the gleaming brass knocker again when Frank restrained him. 'Let's go round the back as he says. No use in upsettin' folk till we find out what we want.'

Grumbling resentfully, Butch allowed Frank to lead him round the side of the house. Another black face opened the door to them. Though this rear entrance man was not dressed to the same standard as was the front-door servant, he too looked upon the saddle bums with the same air of disdain.

'Wait here.'

Again the door was closed upon them.

'Damnit, I'm getting fed up with this.'

As Butch raised his fist to hammer on the door it opened and an attractive black girl, dressed in a maid's outfit, appeared in the opening with a tray. She minced past the bewildered men and set the tray upon a table. As they watched she turned to them and curtsied, then she walked back inside.

'Well I'll be danged.'

The tray contained glasses along with a jug of lemonade that was rimmed with frosting and had pieces of ice floating in the liquid.

'You think that's for us?' Frank whispered reverently.

'Hell I know, but I ain't waiting for no permission to partake.'

They were seated at the table on two cane chairs with brimming glasses when the door opened and an elegantly dressed man emerged. He was a tall man, a few inches over six feet with broad shoulders and piercing eyes. Well into his forties, he was clean-shaven and stood so erect he seemed taller than he actually was.

'Ah, gentlemen, I hope the lemonade is to your liking. My name is Granville Aloysius Garrett Miller. To what do I owe the honour of this pleasurable visit?'

Their host listened attentively to their tale and asked no questions while they talked. Leaving out the detail of their own incarceration during the robbery, Butch told it as if they had ridden up to the way station after the raid. He also told of finding the farmhouse and the murdered couple.

'This girl, she's the only one as can identify them renegades,' the cowboy explained. 'She saw them plain when they murdered her parents.'

At last their host nodded with a slight frown on his face. 'So what you're saying is these desperadoes butchered the travellers at this way station and you have followed them all the way here?'

'That's the long and short of it,' Butch agreed.

'And you also have a witness who can identify these killers?'

'Sure thing; her testimony will hang them killers for sure.'

Butch and Frank waited while the dandy pondered on what they had told them.

'And you wonder what business they had with me?' He eyed them speculatively for a moment before continuing,

'Somehow I think you have the wrong men in your sights. These men you claim were the perpetrators of these atrocities were in actual fact innocent travellers. Strangely enough they had also witnessed the massacre or at least the aftermath of the deed. They managed to rescue my wife from the slaughter and brought her back.' He rose from his seat. 'Let me bring my wife and let her tell you her version of events.'

Granville Aloysius Garrett Miller rose from his chair and bowed to his visitors. As he disappeared indoors Butch and Frank looked at each other with puzzled frowns.

'A mighty strange twist to the tale if you ask me,' Frank observed. 'Do you think we bin mistaken?'

'Danged if I know, old-timer. The whole business is as queer as a two-headed calf.'

A movement to one side drew their attention. One of the black servants was standing in the garden peering at the two men through the carved rails of the veranda. He was scowling at Butch and Frank but what was even more disconcerting was the shotgun he poked between the rails and was pointing at the two men. Before they could react another man appeared from the other side and slid his weapon through the rails to cover them.

'What the . . . ?'

Butch got no further. The door on to the veranda opened and the owner of the house stepped outside. In his hand was a large pistol.

'I want you gentlemen to sit very still. My servants have instructions to shoot at the least sign of any hostile move on your part. My gardeners have been summoned and when they arrive they will relieve you of your weapons.'

16

'Sheriff, these are the fellas as robbed the stage at Empire Fastness Way Station. Caught them red-handed trying to sell some of the loot.'

Granville Aloysius Garrett Miller threw a holdall on top of the sheriff's desk. The contents clinked as it landed.

'Robbed . . . stagecoach . . . way station . . . '

The sheriff was staring with some bewilderment at the people who had descended upon his office on a peaceful afternoon.

'You know, Sheriff — the report that came in this morning of the robbery.' Miller was glaring meaningfully at the lawman. 'The robbery, Sheriff! You know the details that came over the wire this morning.'

'Oh, sure, sure, Mr Miller.'

The sheriff looked as if he had no

idea what Miller was talking about but he was not going to challenge him.

'Hell damnit,' Butch protested, 'we had nothing to do with that robbery, you son of a bitch. You trying to frame us. I've had one run-in with the law what weren't my fault; I ain't going down for something I didn't do.'

'See, Officer, he's admitting to having a criminal record,' Miller exclaimed triumphantly. 'Slap them in jail. We'll send a wire to Wells Fargo we caught the robbers.'

'Consarn it, we ain't no killers nor no robbers. We're trailing them fellas as did the killing. The trail led us here to this goddamn town.'

By now the sheriff was on his feet. Butch and Frank watched helplessly as he produced a bunch of keys from a drawer. They could do nothing for Miller had his servants with him and they kept the two men covered with their shotguns. In a very short time Butch found himself in a similar situation as he had been in Hinkly before being sentenced to prison by Judge Pleasance. His protests were ignored and he was locked in a cell.

'What the hell we gonna do now?' he said plaintively. 'Miller's suckered us into the frame. While those killers walk free we end up in jail with robbery and murder charges hanging over us.'

'That goddamn Miller's in this up to his neck. Them renegades musta brought him the loot from the stage. I reckon he's what's called a fence,' Frank observed dolefully. 'He's cooked our goose good and proper.'

'Hell, we gotta get outta here and pronto. The last time I went afore a judge on false charges I got ten years in the pen. This time I reckon they'll hang me.' The cowboy rubbed a hand around his neck. 'I got too much living to do. I'm too young to die.'

'Dang blame, it don't make it any easier bein' old neither,' answered Frank. 'Where the goddamn hell's Joe?'

The prisoners stared at each other with sudden understanding in their eyes.

'Damnit, say nothing about Joe. Mebby they don't know about him.'

'And worse still, if they think Jessica'll contradict their story then she's in danger. They'll likely as not kidnap her or kill her. Damn that Miller to hell and back.'

★ ★ ★

There was no one at the livery when Jessica arrived back there. She decided to wait and, looking round, found a comfortable pile of straw inside an empty stall. Dolefully she parked herself on this and waited for her new friends. Gradually the stresses and horrific events of the past days took their toll and she fell into a doze.

Men's gruff voices awoke her and at first she thought her companions had returned. But the voices were unfamiliar. The straw was warm and soft beneath her and she lay quietly listening.

'Hey, anyone here? Where the hell's that liveryman?'

'Comin', comin',' an irascible voice answered. 'Can't a fella get no peace around here?'

'We're looking for a bunch of riders come in this afternoon. Had a girl with them. We're looking for the girl. She's run away from home and her ma an' pa wants her taken back.'

Jessica's eyes snapped open, her sleepiness suddenly gone.

'Well, if that don't beat all. Yeah, them fellas did stop here. Got their hosses back there in the corral. Them fellas was enquirin' about a place to stay. I sent them down to Mary Todd's place. If you wanna find that young gal that's the most likely place.'

There was the sound of steps retreating from the livery.

'Well, if that don't beat all, run away from home. Dang kids.' Complaining about the ingratitude of children, the liveryman shuffled back to his cubbyhole.

Jessica slowly sat up. She figured the men were looking for her. For some reason they had made up the story that she was a runaway. Cautiously she stepped out into the main alleyway of the deserted stables as she pondered her next move.

The men looking for her would go to the boarding-house and, not finding her, would go back to their boss for instructions. She would have to go to the big house and tell Butch and Frank about the men looking for her. They would know what to do. Her mind made up, she exited the stables after making sure the men searching for her were nowhere in sight.

She hesitated about approaching the grand house. To her unsophisticated eye the place looked like a palace. Overcoming her nervousness she pushed inside the gates and made her way through the grounds and around the back.

Within the gardens she heard someone humming. An old black man was hoeing the dirt around a large ornamental tree. This activity was reassuringly familiar for Jessica had done the same job on the vegetable patch at home.

'Pardon me, mister, I'm looking for two men who came here a little while ago. Can you tell me where they're at?'

'It's sure a fine day for hoeing, missy.'

'I guess. Did you see those two fellas — one was old like and the other was a younger fella, dressed in cowboy style?'

'It's sure a fine day for hoeing, missy.' The man never ceased his rhythmic movement — the blade of the hoe sliding through the dirt, levelling the almost perfect tilth. 'It's sure a fine day for hoeing,' he repeated.

Jessica glared with some exasperation at the man. Before she could remonstrate with him there was the sound of someone giggling. Jessica whirled around to see a young black girl holding a heaped laundry basket. She was grinning broadly at Jessica.

'You won't get no sense outta old Amos. He gone in the head. Where you from, anyways?'

Jessica joined the young girl and

accompanied her as she began walking deeper into the grounds.

'Me . . . I . . . back a ways, yonder.' Jessica made a vague gesture in the direction of her home. 'I'm looking for two friends of mine. I left them here a while ago.'

The girl's eyes widened. 'You mean those fellas the master took down the jail?'

'Took to jail! What for?'

They had reached the clothesline and the girl put down her basket and started to peg the wet garments in place. Jessica began to help. The black girl looked with some surprise and pleasure as Jessica worked alongside her.

'What for they put them in jail?' Jessica asked again.

'I don't know. Geraint and Thomas and Passer — the master he gave them all guns and they held them fellas till Cess and Tebbet came up and took them fellas' guns. They marched them all down the jail. That's where they at now.'

Jessica stared at her companion. 'What am I gonna do? They were my friends.'

'You come up the house with me. I'll sneak you in back. We'll try and find out what them fellas did to end up in jail. What your name? I'm Ruth.'

Carrying the empty basket the young laundry maid turned and began to walk back towards the house. Jessica trudged beside her, distress showing plainly on her face.

17

Joe was looking with some satisfaction at the little pile of coins on the table in front of him. He was thinking if his luck ran on like this he would accumulate enough to buy his pals a drink when they all met up again.

'Raise a quarter,' a slightly tubby man wearing a brown derby threw his coins into the pot.

There was about four dollars in the centre of the table. Joe was an astute player and he had assessed his opponents around the poker table. He had figured the guy in the derby as a cautious player. The man would not be bluffing. He would have something substantial in his cards to back up his quarter. Joe looked with some regret at the pair of sevens in his hand and decided to fold. He tossed his cards to the table with a wry expression.

'I'm outta this one.'

'I'll see your bet and raise,' the man with the unlit cigar clamped in the corner of his mouth said.

Derby hat was unsure. Joe could see his eyes shift from the pile of coins on the table to his cards. Joe regarded his fellow card players carefully.

This was how you gauged your opponents. By watching their little mannerisms, you assessed their strengths and weaknesses and could tell when someone was bluffing and when they held a good hand. But his attention was distracted by a sudden disturbance behind him. There was the scraping of chairs being pushed back and a flurry of movement.

'Goddamn you to hell, you been cheating all along.'

Joe twisted round to see what was going on. Two of the card players at the next table were on their feet while their companions sat frozen in place. Both the men were armed. Joe sensed the situation could explode into violence.

143

He saw he was in no immediate danger for the men facing each other were to the side of him. If shooting started he was well out of the line of fire. However he made up his mind to fling himself on the floor if things got out of hand.

'Take that back. You accusing me because of your own cheating.'

'I saw you plain. That card came off the bottom of the deck.'

'Look, guys, let's settle this peaceable,' a man at the table with a large walrus moustache pleaded. He may well not have wasted his breath.

'No one accuses me of cheating 'less he can back it up.'

The man accused of cheating wore a small goatee beard and a surly look. His opponent was a young cowboy with a frank open face. The cowboy took a step back from the table.

'I say again you're a miserable, low-down, cheating coyote. You been cheating all night. Just put the money you stole from me and these other fellas on the table and I'll allow you to walk outta here. Otherwise you can be carried out.'

Goatee beard's face twitched as he saw his accuser was not going to back down. 'Damn you, you're just a poor loser. You're more at home with those dumb cows you herd than in civilized company.'

There was a sudden movement as the other players at the table pushed back their chairs and scrambled to get out of the line of fire should shooting break out.

Joe was sitting quietly tensed as he watched the two protagonists. Off to one side of the cowboy he saw a furtive movement. As he watched he saw a man to the forefront of the crowd stealthily pull his side arm. He caught the slight movement of the tinhorn as he signalled the man in the crowd. Suddenly the carpenter realized the young cowboy would not stand a chance against a sneak bullet from behind.

'Watch out behind you, cowboy!' he

yelled, and swivelled round in his chair pulling at his own Colt as he did so.

Everything happened at once. The cowboy went for his iron. His opponent pulled his weapon also. Both fired instantaneously and missed. All around them the onlookers were throwing themselves to the floor or rushing to get out of the way of the stray bullets.

The cowboy dived to the floor and was immediately out of the line of fire from the man he had accused of cheating. Joe saw the man's companion level his pistol at the crouching cowboy. He fired instinctively and saw the man jerk and turn away. Then a shot smashed into the back of his chair. Wood splintered and sprayed into his face. Joe swung around and saw the man with the goatee beard lining up for another shot at him. He thumbed a quick shot at the gunman as he slid from the damaged seat to crouch beside the cowboy. Shots were being fired indiscriminately at the two men cowering on the floor.

'Thanks, friend,' the cowboy panted.

Joe's answer was to curse vehemently as a bullet ploughed a furrow along his arm. 'Goddamn it,' he swore, and rolled away hoping to find refuge from the bullets under his own table. With a quick twist and a kick he overturned the table. Risking a quick look around the side he fired a couple of shots towards the gunman. The man's cronies were joining in and more bullets were coming Joe's way.

'Hell, how did I get involved in this?'

He heard a grunt and glanced across at the cowboy. The youngster was clutching a hand to a bloody shoulder.

'In here!' Joe yelled, and fired a couple of more shots in the direction of the gunmen. His hammer clicked on an empty shell. 'Damnit.'

He lay on his side and quickly began to reload from his belt. There was a groan nearby. It came from the cowboy. Joe could only see the lower half of the youngster. The legs kicked out and then went ominously still.

'Fella, you all right?' Joe called.

There was no answer. The cowboy remained motionless. Joe guessed the cowboy was out of the action. Bullets thudded into the woodwork of the table. He glanced round wildly looking for some escape from the dire situation he now found himself in. Nothing obvious presented itself. With his freshly loaded Colt he poked a cautious head over the top of the table.

Bullets thudded into the table and buzzed past his exposed head. The cardsharp's cronies had joined the fight. Joe was well outnumbered.

He dropped back to the floor and thumbed a few shots in the general direction of the assailants. Desperately he searched round for a way out of this impasse. He eyed the table behind which he crouched. Suddenly he saw a possibility.

'The round table,' he grunted.

Grasping a sturdy leg he began to rotate the table. There were yells of frustration from his attackers. The barrage of shots seemed to intensify. Joe could feel the table shuddering as bullets thudded into the wood.

'Don't let the goddamn sonofabitch get away!'

The table came to a halt as it came up against the solid construction of the bar. Joe took a deep breath, reached over the table and without looking emptied his Colt into the saloon. Almost as the hammer struck the last shell Joe leapt up and flung himself on to the top of the bar.

He half-rolled, half-skidded across the polished wood. Abruptly he reached the other side and was over and falling. He could hear bullets smashing into the glass bottles lined up behind the bar. At the end of the bar he saw the door. On hands and knees he scrambled towards this. Not knowing if it was locked or not he took a chance and flung himself at the door.

For a few breathtaking moments the door held. Bullets were now tracing a pattern on the door panels. Then the door opened under Joe's frantic pushing and he fell through. From a prone position he kicked the door shut and quickly scrambling to his feet he ran down a gloomy passageway. Another door barred his way. Joe threw his not inconsiderable bulk at the door. After the second attempt his shoulder burst the door open and Joe was outside and fleeing down an alleyway.

He ran towards the rear of the buildings. Some minutes later he was crouching inside an old outhouse. Trying to quieten his breathing he strained to listen for sounds of pursuit. He heard shouts in the distance but the disturbance seemed well away from his refuge.

'Damn me,' he muttered, 'it seems every time I get in a card game I end up in trouble.'

He pushed out spent shells and reloaded, then sat quietly while he thought out his next move. The hullabaloo seemed to have died down and Joe eased out of his hiding place and warily made his way back to the street.

'Well I ain't made much progress with my enquiries,' he mused. 'I guess by now they'll all be waiting down at the livery for me.'

18

Jessica sat at the kitchen table. The wooden surface was scrubbed almost white. She sipped from a large mug of coffee. On the table in front of her was a plate of cookies. Looking around her Jessica reckoned the kitchen of the big house was almost as big as the whole of her old house where she had lived with her father and mother.

An obese black woman worked at a huge iron stove. She hummed gently to herself as she moved pots and skillets around with a dexterity born of long experience. Occasionally she would glance at the young white girl and smile at her. Jessica looked up with some relief when the door opened and Ruth came in.

'Those friends of yours robbed the stage and murdered the passengers. Geraint says they even brought with them the things they stole and wanted to sell them to master Miller.'

Jessica was staring with some puzzlement at her new friend. 'When were they took to jail?'

'Just about an hour or so back. Geraint reckons they'll hang.'

'That can't be right. We were told the men as did do the robbery had come here to see Mr Miller. Those same men came by our ranch and murdered my ma and pa. Butch and Frank ain't no robbers. What am I gonna do? They the only friends I got.'

'Your ma and pa murdered — oh my! Geraint says the master is looking for a young girl as is run away. Is that you?'

'Yes,' Jessica said in a low trembling voice. 'I don't know what is happening.'

Before she could continue the door opened and the master of the house walked into the kitchen. Two men accompanied him — the same two who had helped take Butch and Frank prisoner.

'Well, well, isn't this fortunate — the

young runaway. We'll have to keep you safe till your parents come to collect you.'

Jessica made a quick dash for the door. The cook saw her coming and stepped in front of her. Jessica cannoned into the woman. The cook was much softer than the wall of the house but just as immovable. Jessica was stopped short and a pair of meaty arms was wrapped round her. Struggle as she might there was no escaping that embrace. The two male servants took hold of her and began the task of dragging the kicking, struggling girl from the kitchen.

'Come along now, miss,' Miller said. 'Your ma and pa are out of their minds worrying about you. They're desperate to have you back in the bosom of the family.'

'It's a lie,' she yelled, as she fought her captors. 'My ma and pa were killed. Butch and Frank were looking after me . . . '

Despite her struggles she was taken

upstairs and locked in one of the many bedrooms. As the door was closed and locked she flung herself against it and banged and kicked at the solid wood.

'Let me out. You can't keep me here.'

But the door remained closed and at last she desisted. Like a trapped animal she paced the room looking for a way out. She tried the windows but they were locked and at last she sat on the bed and wondered what was going to become of her. She had no idea why the lie was being put out that she was a runaway. As she desperately rummaged about for an explanation a remark made by Frank came back to her.

'He said I was a witness to murder,' she said aloud.

But why would the rich and powerful Mr Miller believe she was a runaway?

* * *

The livery looked deserted when Joe entered by the main doors. Then there was a movement from inside. A man moved out from one of the stalls.

'Hello, is that you, Butch?' the ex-carpenter called.

'No, it ain't Butch. You a friend of his?'

Too late Joe noticed the gun in the man's hand. 'What the hell's this, mister? I want no trouble. I'm just looking for some friends of mine. We were supposed to meet up here. Why the gun?'

'Jess, I reckon this is one of them rannies the boss told us to round up,' the man called.

Joe heard a movement behind him.

'OK, mister, just shuck your gun. We're taking you down the jail.'

'Jail!' Joe protested. 'What the hell am I supposed to have done?'

'From what we make out, you and your pals robbed the stage at Empire Fastness Way Station and killed every man, woman and child. We got your buddies down in the jail right now. We gonna string you up along with your murdering pals. Now do as Jess says and shuck that hardware.'

Joe had one taste of Western justice and that was enough to last him a lifetime. He knew there was no way he was going back to jail.

'I reckon you got me dead to rights.' As he spoke he reached for his Colt as if about to give it up.

'Careful, no false moves.'

Joe pulled his Colt and at the same time threw himself into the opening of the stall. Guns blasted as the men who had apprehended him fired a fraction too late. There was a scream from one of the men.

Joe risked a peek over the wall of the stall. The one he reckoned was called Jess was sitting in the straw clutching a revolver against his chest. An ominous red stain was spreading over his shirt. Joe quickly turned his attention to the first man. He was staring at his sidekick with a shocked look on his face. His pistol hung limply from his hand.

'Goddamn it, Jess, I never meant — '

'Drop that pistol!' Joe yelled, and

fired over the gunman's head.

The man jerked with shock and tore his eyes from his wounded companion.

'Drop it now!' Joe shouted again. 'You're a dead man if you don't.'

The gun thudded to the floor. Cautiously Joe stepped out from the stall. 'See to Jess,' he ordered.

While the man stumbled forward to the wounded Jess, Joe collected the discarded Colt. He tucked it in his waistband. As he stood up, the first attacker made a grab for the Colt still clutched in Jess's blood-covered hand. Joe swore and instinctively fired. The bullet hit the man in the side of the head and he toppled over. For a few moments his legs kicked at the straw-covered floor and then all the movement ceased. Jess was staring at his dead companion.

'Jesus, you killed him.'

Joe stalked forward. 'Everyone in this town is goddamned trigger-happy. I just had to shoot my way outta the Good Eva Arcadia 'cause I tried to help a cowboy in trouble.'

He crouched down in front of the wounded man, trying his best to ignore the body of the man he had just shot. 'Let me have a look, Jess.'

Dark blood was oozing from the centre of the man's chest. Joe looked round for something to staunch the bleeding. The only thing that came readily to hand was the dead man's bandanna. He opened the blood-saturated shirt and pushed the wadded cloth inside.

'You need a doctor, Jess. I'll get someone to help you. But first tell me why you were lying in wait for me.'

'Go to hell! You just shot Louis. I ain't telling you nothing.'

Joe sighed and sat back on his heels. 'In that case there's no hope for you. I won't fetch no doctor. So there's a good chance you'll bleed to death. Anyways I can't see why you're so loyal to a fella as just shot you.'

'Damn you to hell! We work for Mr Miller. He told us they'd tracked down the men as robbed the stage and murdered all those people. We were to be on the lookout for a young girl that was running with them. She's run away from home and her ma wants her back.'

'Louis here said my friends were in jail. Who accused them of the robbery?'

'Listen, mister, this is hurting real bad. Get that sawbones. I don't wanna die in no stable.'

'Just answer my questions. Who accused them of the killings at Empire Fastness?'

'Mr Miller did. He caught them when they went up his place to try and sell the stolen goods. His men got the drop on them and marched them down the jail. He told me and Louis to look for the girl. We figured she would be coming back to the livery.'

'This Miller fella, where's his place at?'

'Big house . . . south of town . . . can't miss it. Got them pillars and big gardens . . . '

The man's voice faded and his head

slumped forward.

'Jess, Jess.' Joe felt for a pulse. 'Damn me, if this ain't the goddamndest unhealthiest town. Couple of fellas dead in the saloon and now two more in the livery. The sooner I can figure a way to bust Butch and Frank outta jail and find Jessica the sooner we can shake the dust of this damned place.'

19

For reasons best known to himself the liveryman did not come to investigate the shooting. He may have thought it prudent to keep well clear of such incidents. The livery was far enough from the main township for the gunshots to have been missed so no one else came to investigate.

When he realized he was not going to be disturbed, Joe helped himself to the men's weapons. He was about to hide the bodies inside an empty stall when an idea began to take shape. His next move was to go outside to the corral and saddle up their mounts. Concealing the two pistols that had belonged to the dead men inside his coat, he mounted one of the horses and rode back to town.

He soon spotted the sheriff's office and steeling himself for another shoot-out, he breezed inside.

The sheriff of Coventree was a handsome, florid individual. The traces of his fine features were being submerged in fat that good living and indolence brought to the majority of men as they slid into middle age. He looked up from the newspaper he had been reading when Joe walked in.

'Howdy, Sheriff, you in charge here?'

'Well, can you see anybody else in here?'

'Sheriff, I don't know what kinda town this is but I just rode in and was about to put my horse in the livery when I got the dangdest shock. There's two dead bodies lying there. I tell you, man, I lit outta there as fast as my horse could take me.'

'The hell you say! What's got into this town! Earlier on there was a shooting down at the Good Eva Arcadia. Damnit, if this goes on I'll take early retirement.' The sheriff stood and belted on a holster. 'Come on, fella, show me where these bodies are.'

'Sheriff, I ain't going back there no

how. I'm heading for a good stiff drink. I ain't used to finding dead bodies. Where would be a safe place to go for a quiet drink?'

'Damnit man, if they're dead they can't hurt none.' The sheriff frowned suddenly. 'You wait here till I investigate this. I might need you as witness.'

Grabbing his hat, the sheriff walked out slamming the door behind him. Joe blinked in some bewilderment at the success of his ploy.

'Just shows the simpler the plan the better.'

Rummaging around in the desk he found a bunch of keys. Mixed in with the keys were a couple of spare badges. With a grin Joe pinned one on his coat.

There were two prisoners in one cell and Butch and Frank in a separate one. They all looked up as Joe entered. Grinning widely the big man sauntered up to the cells.

'You them dangerous criminals what I gotta take out for hanging?' he said impishly.

'Joe!'

'Sure as shooting, it's good old reliable Joe Peters.' Joe unlocked the cell door. 'Have you any last requests before I take you out and hang you?'

The cowboy was out of the cell and hugging his partner. 'How the hell did you wangle this?'

'Butch, I'm the brains of this outfit and don't you forget it. Come on.'

He handed out the pistols. Frank and Butch grabbed one each and they all headed out to the front of the jail.

'Make your way down to the livery,' Joe instructed the released prisoners as he mounted his horse. 'But be careful. The sheriff is down there. We may have to grab him to keep him from raising the alarm.'

The sheriff was in deep discussion with the liveryman when they arrived. When the three fugitives walked into the stables with drawn guns both men gave in without a fight.

'Goddamn, you fellas are headed for a hanging,' the sheriff spluttered as

Butch relieved him of his side arm.

'What we gonna do with them?' Butch asked.

'Why don't we take them back down the jail and lock them in?' suggested Joe. 'That way no one will find them for a while. Give us a chance to go down this Miller's place and get some answers.'

'Hell,' Frank crowed, 'I ain't never put no one in jail afore. I been put in myself a times but this'll make a welcome change.'

'Sheriff, we'll walk down the jail together. We'll have guns on you all the time we're walking. You wanna live to enjoy your retirement you walk like you are escorting us and not the other way around.'

It was agreed that Joe would go on to the Miller place and when Butch and Frank had the prisoners safely stowed they would meet up at the banker's mansion.

'I reckon that coyote owes us a few answers. On your way back from the jail bring the horses,' Joe instructed. 'They're all saddled and ready. We'll meet round the back of the place.'

Bearing in mind the treatment Butch and Frank had received at the hands of the banker, Joe rode around to the rear of the mansion seeking some access to the house.

A sturdy wooden fence constructed from untrimmed logs driven into the dirt kept the riff-raff from invading the grounds. Joe was studying this barricade when he heard hoofbeats. He loosened his Colt in the holster but there was no need for alarm. The horsemen were Butch and Frank arriving as arranged.

'How the hell we gonna get over that?' Joe asked indicating the fence.

Edging his mount close, Butch loosed his rope and with no great effort lassoed an upright. Wrapping the rope around his saddle horn the cowboy urged his horse back from the fence. The rope tightened then with a terrific groan a whole section gave way.

Joe was staring with admiration at the destruction. 'Well, I'll be . . . that's one way of gaining unlawful entry.'

Once inside the grounds they dismounted and tethered their horses amongst trees well out of sight of the house. Joe unlimbered the shotgun he had taken from the way station.

'You say those fellas throwed down on you with shotguns. Let's see how they like one pointed in their direction.'

Cautiously they moved out and advanced through the shrubbery in the direction of the house. No one challenged them and in a short time they were at the back porch.

'Frank, you stay out here and watch for trouble while Butch and I go inside. If you hear shooting come running.'

Butch and Joe looked at each other and nodded. Joe kicked in the back door and went through the opening at a run. Butch dodged inside behind Joe and they found themselves in a passageway that ran towards the front of the house.

20

'Check each door as we go. You take the right side and I'll take the left.'

Before they had advanced very far a door opened and the liveried servant who had slammed the front door on Butch and Frank on their first visit stood gawking at the two intruders.

'Ah, my fine friend,' the cowboy called, as he covered the man with his Colt. 'Make a false move and I'll blow your goddamned head off. Where is your master, Mr Big Shot Miller?'

'I . . . I . . . he's not here.' The man stood very still.

Joe pushed past the man and stepped inside. The room was furnished as a study with a desk and bookshelves lining the walls. On the desk stood a decanter with a dark liquid and a partially filled glass. Butch pushed the servant into the room none too gently.

'Looks like our friend here was helping himself to the brandy,' Joe said, sniffing at the glass. He tossed off the contents. 'Now that is what I call brandy. Get some more glasses.'

Trembling with fear the man did as instructed and filled the tumblers.

'Butch, find out what you can from this dressed-up monkey while I take this drink out to Frank.'

The cowboy took a long pull before turning to the servant. 'First off my friend, I had a fine pair of Remington pistols that have sentimental value. I want them back.'

'All guns are in the gunroom.'

Butch held up his glass and the servant obediently refilled it. Joe came in and also had a refill.

'He's got the guns they took from Frank and me in the gunroom. I want my stuff back.'

'Right, but first we need to know who's here and when Miller is expected back.' Joe pushed the shotgun under the servant's chin. 'I must tell you this thing has a hair trigger. It goes off if it senses a lie forming in any deceitful throat. Now who else is in the house and where is your master?'

There was a look of abject terror on the man's face as he stared into the big man's grim face. 'Master is down at the bank. He always go there. The servants look after everything. We ain't gonna cause you no bother, mister.'

'Too right, my friend, any bother will get you good and dead.'

There was a noise at the door and the two intruders whirled with their weapons pointing at Frank as he stood on the entrance with an empty glass.

'I was hopin' for some more of that there brandy.'

'Goddamn it, Frank, you're supposed to be on lookout,' Joe fulminated.

'Where's the kitchen?' Butch interjected, as he filled up his tumbler from the decanter now almost empty. 'And find us some more of this here brandy.'

'The kitchen?' Joe frowned at his friend.

'Hell's bell, Joe, I can't remember the last time I ate.'

'Goddamn thinking of your belly and any moment now Miller will be about our necks with half the town behind him.'

While they argued the servant produced two bottles of brandy.

'Here,' Joe handed one of the bottles to Frank. 'Now get out there and keep a watch.'

A row of black faces turned to the door as Joe and Butch ushered in the fancy dressed servant. Three men and a couple of women were sitting at a loaded table. The smell of cooking filled the spacious kitchen.

'Just in time for dinner,' Joe chuckled, as he sauntered over to the table and helped himself to a cut of beef.

'You're Jessica's friends.'

Butch stared at the young girl who spoke. 'Jessica? Sure thing, how come you know Jessica?'

'She upstairs locked in a room. Master Miller, he had her put there.'

Butch turned and hit the liveried servant a clout on the side of the head with his pistol. 'You sonofabitch, you weren't gonna tell me about Jessica.'

The man staggered back from the irate cowboy, rubbing at his injured head. 'Master, I was just about to tell you about the girl,' he whined. 'Don't hit me no more.'

Butch shoved the Colt into the man's midriff. 'You take me this minute to that room. Any more lies and I'll blow a hole in your guts and watch you expire. Joe, you see what else you can find from these people. Don't go easy on them. Some of them held Frank and me at gunpoint and handed us over to that sheriff. Just shoot anyone that looks like trouble.'

Butch gripped the servant he had hit and pushed him roughly towards the door. As they left Joe pointed his shotgun at the diners.

'I'm gonna ask questions. You tell me what I wanna know and you might just live to carry on serving your master.'

Upstairs, the frightened manservant led Butch to a bedroom door. He produced a key and, unlocking the door, stepped aside for Butch to precede him. Butch grinned.

'You think I'm that stupid?'

He grabbed the man's shoulder and pushed him roughly ahead of him. There was a startled yelp and the man collapsed on to the carpeted floor. Broken crockery showered to the carpet and Jessica darted into the doorway. She pulled up short as she saw Butch. In her hand was the handle of a water jug, which was all that remained of the instrument she had used to crown the servant.

'You!'

Butch was grinning at her. 'That was a pretty good strike. Good job I let him go first.' He stepped inside and dragged the groaning man clear of the door. 'We'll lock the sonofabitch in here, then we can join Joe downstairs.'

They found Joe sitting at the dining-table with a plate of meat and a glass of wine in front of him. Beside him was propped his shotgun.

'Jessica.' Joe waved expansively around the table. 'Grab yourselves a seat and have a bite to eat. Have I got a curious tale to relate.'

Shaking her head in bewilderment the girl did as she was told and sat while Ruth, the young woman who had befriended her, served them with a jug of milk and a plate heaped with sliced meats. All this time the members of the staff sat around the table in frightened silence.

'I think I got the right of it,' Joe continued, when both Jessica and Butch were seated at the table and had been served. 'A banker from back East arrived at the house. Then the gossip is that he and Miller's wife legged it on that stage what we saw stalled at Empire Fastness. From what I can gather this banker fella was transferring funds to the bank in Brimingdam. As we know, the banker never made it. The stage was ambushed at Empire Fastness

Way Station and everyone killed. The strange thing is that one person survived that raid.' Joe paused and supped at his wine.

'Who?' Butch snapped. 'For God's sake, tell us who!'

'Mrs Miller. From what I can gather the fellas we been tracking brought her back.'

'One of us oughta relieve Frank while we tell him of this,' Butch mumbled indistinctly, as he crammed meat into his mouth. 'Maybe he can make sense of it all. Sure baffles me.'

'I say we recover our weapons and stock up on food and then get as far away from this place as possible.'

There was a flurry of shots from the front of the house as Joe spoke. The three friends looked at each other with alarm.

'It's from out front. Frank must be in trouble.'

Joe grabbed up his shotgun and ran from the kitchen. He paused and flattened against the wall. Cautiously he pointed the shotgun towards the front door. The door was open and Frank was lying in the hallway cursing roundly with blood welling up from a wound in his side.

21

Taking in the situation Joe fired both barrels of his shotgun through the open doorway to discourage anyone from invading the house. There was a yell outside and bullets poured into the hallway. Crawling forward, Joe gripped Frank by his shoulder and dragged him from the open door. The old-timer grunted as another bullet hit him in the leg. In the hall behind Joe, Butch opened up with his Colt, shooting through the open front door.

'How is Frank?' he yelled at Joe.

'Been hit a couple of times. We gotta get him outta here.'

'How are you, old-timer?'

'I bin worse. Don't worry about me. You lot light outta here. Leave me. I'll stand them off while you get out the back.'

'No way, old man. You're coming

with us,' Butch replied. 'I've sent Jessica to recover our guns. Let's drag this old coot back from the doorway.'

Bullets were still coming into the hall but the partners kept low and most of the lead passed harmlessly overhead. They pulled the wounded man in the direction of the kitchen.

'Goddamn it, leave me alone and stop draggin' me like a roped steer.'

Ignoring the wounded man's pleas they managed to get him inside the kitchen. The servants were lying on the floor looking more scared than ever. Joe grabbed some cloths hanging by the big stove and tied these round the wounds.

'That should stem the bleeding till we get him to safety.'

Jessica and the young black girl arrived loaded down with guns and ammunition.

'Well done,' Joe applauded the girls. 'We'll get out the back and try and make it to the horses. We may have to shoot our way out.' In spite of the old-man's protests Joe tugged Frank to his feet. 'Listen, old-timer, we can't leave you here. They're liable to hang you for those killings they wanna pin on us. Let's go!'

Butch had strapped Sheriff Patterson's Remington Colts around his waist. The cowboy had become quite attached to the matched pistols and was glad to have them in his possession once more. He felt he could face anything with those weapons. Jessica followed the men, carrying a rifle in each hand. As well as giving Butch back his prized weapons she also handed him a Remington rifle. He grinned at her.

'Just call me the Remington Kid.'

At the rear door Joe supported the wounded Frank while Butch poked the door open with his rifle. Shots hammered into the doorway.

'Goddamn it,' Butch cursed.

He laid the rifle on the floor and stepped close to the open door. Bullets were splintering chips of wood from the frame. Butch drew the twin pistols and dropping to one knee he risked a look outside. The pistols bucked in his hands as he picked targets and emptied all twelve bullets at the men crouching on the lawn outside. There were screams and curses and the firing from outside ceased abruptly. Butch rammed his empty weapons back in the holsters and grabbed up the rifle. With a sudden leap he was outside on the back porch and taking rapid pot shots at the fleeing men.

'Come on, fellas,' he called. 'We got them on the run.'

Jessica came first with Joe following — the big man almost carrying the groaning Frank.

'Keep going. I'll cover you.'

Jessica followed Joe and Frank. Behind them came Butch firing off an occasional round in an attempt to keep their attackers from rallying. They made it to the shrubbery without further injury.

'Keep going. Keep going,' Butch urged his companions.

They weren't likely to hesitate now

that they were out of the house and had a chance to reach their mounts. Then they were in amongst the trees and could see the horses where they had left them.

'Can you ride, Frank?'

'Just get me on top of that nag and I'll hang on,' Frank said through gritted teeth.

Miller's mansion was on the outskirts of the town and they rode hard for the open country. A few desultory shots winged their way when they broke cover but soon they left the buildings behind. As they hit open country they were riding as hard as was possible with a wounded Frank grimly gripping the reins and slumped over the neck of his mount. The ground was gradually rising and they saw the hills in the distance.

'We'll head for those hills,' Joe called. 'I reckon they'll get a posse together and come after us. We'll have to ride as long as Frank can keep up.'

There was no response from the old man. Glancing at him Joe could see the lines of pain deeply etched on his features. His hands looked as bloodless as peeled twigs as they clasped the reins in a death-like grip.

'Goddamn that Miller to hell and back,' the big man swore under his breath.

The wounded man needed a saw-bones and care and rest. Instead he was on the back of a horse riding for the distant hills. Joe kept glancing back expecting to see a band of horsemen in pursuit.

They rode hard for an hour before easing off to let the horses recover. There was still no sign of the posse but they knew there would be men after them — men with rifles and well-rested horses.

Miller would feed the posse lies about the people they were after. He would fire them up by telling them of the desperate men who had murdered the inhabitants at Empire Fastness Way Station and robbed and killed the passengers and crew of the stagecoach.

Joe looked round at the little band. Butch was riding steady keeping his eyes to the front, alert to any danger. Jessica rode with a determined expression. Frank was hanging on grimly to his blood-soaked reins. The big man sighed deeply.

A few weeks ago he had been a simple carpenter willing to work hard to make a future for his family out West. Circumstances had dictated differently. A thief had purloined his tools; the game of cards that had been meant to regain the means to purchase more tools had resulted in him becoming a killer, facing a ten-year prison sentence; now he was riding for his life with a badly wounded man and a young girl.

He glanced across at Butch. At times thoughtless and reckless, nevertheless when the going got tough the cowboy was a rock in a sea of troubles.

22

They were at least half an hour from the beginning of the foothills before they saw any signs of pursuit.

'Looks like they got the posse after us,' Butch called.

The riders turned and watched the dust cloud. A goodly part of the day had passed and shadows were growing longer.

'Caves ... there's caves in those hills,' Frank panted. 'We find a cave and mebby hole up.'

They turned their eyes front and concentrated on riding. From time to time one of the fugitives would glance behind. The dust cloud following them did not seem to get any closer but they drew no comfort from that.

For all of them it was a scary situation. None of them had been chased like this before. A posse of armed men was pursuing them. If they caught them up there would be shooting. The men after them had no qualms about throwing down on Frank as he stood lookout back at Miller's mansion. Now the townsfolk had drawn blood they would be after more.

The little group kept on riding. Each of them was haunted by the fear of the inevitable showdown that would ensue should they be overtaken. All realized they were keeping their own speed down to the slowest rider. Frank must have recognized this for he urged them to leave him and ride on without him.

'When you reach the hills keep bendin' to the right,' he croaked. 'You'll come across some old mine workin's. There's a hill behind that's got caves. Just go on and save yourselves.'

'We ain't gonna abandon you, old-timer. We all stick together,' Butch asserted. 'We'll outrun those galoots. Just you hang on in there.'

Shortly after that they hit a canyon

and rode through tall pines, the air feeling cold as daylight shortened. The smell of pine and dust lingered in the air. Eventually they began to see waste heaps from the mines.

Nature had been hard at work trying to cover over the scars inflicted on these hills and canyons. Weeds and immature saplings had thrust up from the ramparts of the spoil heaps — beginning to re-establish the more pleasing garment of greenery.

'Keep goin',' Frank whispered feebly as he saw where they had arrived. 'Beyond that hogback is another hill. That's where the caves is at.'

Gaping wounds had been bored into the hills where men had grubbed for silver now long since run out. They rode past the ugly workings that reminded Joe of some old burial place. He imagined the dark holes bored into the solid rock held the remains of an older race. Then once more they were riding through a forest of pines and aspens. Here and there a few giant walnut trees towered above their smaller woodland brothers.

'Not much further now, old-timer,' Joe assured Frank, more for his own comfort.

There was no response. The wounded man was slumped on top of his horse — kept there only because the horses were moving slowly as they threaded through the trees.

They saw the dark holes in the distant rock face as they came out of the trees. Riding over a rocky plateau they arrived at the bottom of the hill. Zigzag trails, looking faintly luminescent in the fading light, led upwards.

Butch pushed ahead and began the ascent. Behind him Joe dismounted and handed his reins to Jessica. Her pale face stared out at him from beneath her battered hat.

'I'm worried Frank will take a fall on the way up,' he explained. 'How he kept on top of that horse is a mystery. I'll lead his mount and make sure he don't fall off.'

Jessica nodded, too tired to make any reply.

It was a fraught climb for them all. The horses did not like the narrow rocky trail they were forced to mount. At times it grew steep and loose stones broke away, falling back down the hillside. The sound of the tumbling rocks was like thunder in their ears. They imagined the posse looking up as they chased into the hills and grinning knowingly at each other.

Butch reached the first of the openings. He could see nothing as he peered into the dim interior.

'This do?' the cowboy asked.

'Maybe push on a little higher.' Joe suggested. 'If the posse get this far we may be safer further on.'

Butch urged his tired horse to climb further. Eventually they settled on a cave that was as big as a single room cabin. By then they were several hundred feet from the base of the hill.

Despondently they led the horses inside, the clatter of hoofs echoing eerily inside the cavern. Frank slipped sideways from his precarious perch atop his horse. Joe who had been supporting him for the duration of the climb was able to catch the wounded man in his brawny arms and ease him to the floor of the cave.

'For better or worse, old-timer, we've arrived at our hideout,' he said, as he propped his wounded companion against the rocky wall of the cave.

Frank made no reply. His face seemed drained of colour.

'Let's get a blanket to make Frank more comfortable. Then we can take care of those wounds.'

They peeled the blood-soaked cloths from the old man's side and from the wound on his leg. Neither looked serious but a lot of blood had leaked into the makeshift bandages and transferred to his clothes. Joe examined the wounds critically.

'That side wound looks bad. I think the bullet is still in there. We'll havta clean both wounds and get that bullet out.' He looked round helplessly at their primitive surrounds. 'We need a fire and some clean bandages. Fat chance while we're holed up here.'

'I grabbed up all the towels from that kitchen,' Jessica confessed.

She began to unpack her saddlebags, pulling out towel after towel and handing them to Joe.

'Jessica, you're a true frontier girl,' Joe said, not hiding his admiration for the girl's foresight.

While Joe helped Jessica with Frank, the cowboy unsaddled the horses.

'Sorry, fellas, there's no feed, but if that liveryman was doing his job he shoulda fed you.'

'Butch, you check for water in those water bottles.'

'What about food?' the cowboy asked, as he collected the canteens.

'We ain't got any.'

Again it was Jessica who came to the rescue. 'I grabbed up this loaf and a side of ham afore we fled the house.'

'Jessica,' Joe pronounced, 'if I weren't

already married I'd ask your hand in marriage right now.'

The darkness of the cave hid the girl's blushes. They shared out the meagre rations, slicing the meat and bread with their knives. They sat quietly around their wounded companion, cold and cheerless. They ate without talking, each lost in their own morbid thoughts.

23

'Bring her down the cellar.'

The young black girl struggled in the grip of the two burly servants. Her eyes rolled wildly as she pleaded with Miller.

'Master, I ain't done nothing wrong.'

The banker ignored the girl's pleas. 'Geraint, go to the stables and fetch me a bullwhip. And hurry, man.'

Geraint ran down the hallway. Ruth was pulled along still protesting. Miller sauntered along behind whistling softly. The cellar door was unlocked and Ruth hesitated at the entrance. A flight of wooden stairs could be seen plunging into the dim interior.

'Please, Master, what you gonna do to me?'

Miller nodded to the male servant and Ruth's speech ended in a shriek as a brutal hand in the flat of her back pushed her inside. Her arms flailed wildly as she tried to keep her balance. A boot on her rear end helped her on her way.

She fell down the stairs, bouncing against each step to the bottom. Miller and his servant entered and began the descent. Ruth sprawled at the bottom of the steps sobbing bitterly.

Without being told, the black man began to light the lanterns hung on the sturdy stanchions that supported the floors above.

Miller walked slowly along the cellar floor ostensibly examining the neat rows of barrels stacked on their sides. The ends of the barrels were decorated with stencilled lettering indicating the contents along with a date. There were barrels of brandy, whiskey and gin of varying vintage. On the other side of the cellar facing the barrels were racks of bottled liquors.

Before the task of lighting the cellar was finished there was the clatter of booted feet on the stairs and Geraint came into the cellar carrying a coiled whip. All this while Ruth lay where she had fallen, sobbing bitterly. Taking the bullwhip from Geraint, Miller nodded towards the weeping girl.

'Tie her to one of the posts.'

The men dragged the whimpering servant-girl across the hard-packed dirt floor and pushed her roughly against an upright. They pulled her arms around the crude beam and fastened her hands with twine to a stout nail. She hung there, her young body quivering in her distress.

As the men finished securing the girl, Miller walked forward and passed the whip to Geraint. The big black man loosed the coils of the whip. In the flickering lights of the dim cavern the loop moved back and forth like a snake with a life independent of the hand holding it.

'Ruth, I am punishing you because you betrayed my trust. You are my servant. Your parents sold you to me. I bought you for fifty dollars. I own you, body and soul. Your loyalty lies with me. I am your lord and master. It is only because of my beneficence that you eat at my table and sleep within the security of my house.'

He nodded and Geraint immediately flicked his wrist. The whip cracked obediently with the movement. Ruth's cries intensified.

'I done nothing wrong, Master,' she wailed. 'Please believe me. I would never do nothing to hurt you, Master.'

' 'For the son dishonoureth the father, the daughter rises up against her mother, the daughter-in-law against her mother-in-law; a man's enemies are the people of his own house'. From the book of Micah,' Miller intoned.

'Ruth, you gave succour to mine enemies. I want you to tell me all about those people that came into my home and violated it. I want the names of the men and the girl also. I want to know what you told them that brought them back to my house. You co-operate and your punishment will be less severe.'

Up in the kitchen the big cook

paused as she kneaded a sizeable slab of raw dough and cocked her head to one side. From somewhere deep within the bowels of the house she fancied she could hear someone screaming.

'Sounds like some poor gal in childbirth,' she mumbled. 'But that ain't likely. Master allus calls me in for that.'

Leaving the table where she had been working she walked across to the door and, opening it, stuck her head outside. Another black servant was standing in the corridor. He turned scared eyes towards the door as he heard it open.

'Thomas, what on earth's goin' on? Sounds like someone's strangulating a cat.'

'It's Ruth, de Massa he done got her down in de cellar.'

'Ruth!' The cook's eyes opened wide. 'What's goin' on? What they doin' to the poor thing?'

The man rolled his eyes in his distress.

'I saw Geraint take a bullwhip from

de stables. When I asked him what for he hit me with it and tole me mind my own gawddamn business.'

For long suspended moments the man and woman stared at each other. The faint screams licked at their consciousness like pale shadows of pain.

'Lord Gawd almighty, what's the world comin' to! The Master wouldn't whip that poor gal, I doan think.'

'I reckon it's 'cause she help dem fellas as cause all de trouble. She tole 'em about de young gal locked upstairs what de Master was keepin' prisoner an' showed dem where de guns is kept. Someone musta blabbed about her. I never seen Master Miller in such a rage as when he come in de house after dem fellas fled. He reckon dey de killingst murderers as he ever come across. He say every way de go dey leave a trail of dead bodies. He sent de sheriff out with a posse huntin' dem. Dey'll hang dem sure as I stand here.'

They heard footsteps approaching.

The cook, moving quickly for such a big woman, disappeared back into her kitchen. There were footsteps in the corridor and she heard her master's voice issuing instructions to his servants.

'Upstairs, put her in the same room that girl was locked in.'

There was the scuffle of boots as men moved off towards the back stairs. The door into the kitchen opened and Miller stepped inside.

'Edna, finish whatever you're doing and get some hot water and dressings for Ruth. I had to discipline the stupid girl for disloyal behaviour. She's got a sore back. Maybe some ointment as well.'

'Sure, Master Miller, I can leave this dough to rise while I tend to her. Where she at?'

'Geraint and Passer have taken her upstairs. Geraint will show you where. When you finished I want everyone gathered in the kitchen here and that means garden staff as well.'

Edna heard the sobbing as she approached the bedroom. Geraint, a big man well over six foot tall with a deep, broad chest, was inside the room glaring balefully at the injured girl. Ruth was lying on her face on the bed sobbing softly into the covers. Her torn blouse showed traces of blood.

'Lordy, Lordy,' the cook exclaimed, 'what a racket.' She nodded to Geraint. 'I'll take care of her now, Geraint. The Master wants us all in the kitchen when I finish here.'

The servant turned his broad brutal face towards the cook. 'Don't be too gentle. She's a bad'un. Master oughta get rid on her.'

'Doan you worry none, Geraint, the Master he do what's right. Now go you and tell everyone to gather at the kitchen. I'll be quick as I can.'

Edna drew in a sharp breath as she saw the state of the girl's back. Long ugly wheals crisscrossed the girl's torso.

'There, there Ruth,' she said gently. 'I

got me some balm here as will ease your pain some. But you gonna be sore for some days.'

The gathering in the large kitchen was a sombre one. Without exception Miller employed only blacks. He ruled them with a rod of iron. His servants worked hard and they worked cheap and as long as they obeyed the rules they had a job at the big house.

His bodyguard Geraint — a man of brutal disposition — enforced discipline. Punishment was usually a beating or for more minor misdemeanours the docking of money from wages.

Miller enjoyed the power he wielded over his servants. Before emancipation his family had owned slaves and Miller resented the upheaval that had demolished that institution. It was slight compensation for that loss that he now employed these servants and disciplined them as he did.

''Every kingdom divided against itself is brought to desolation; and every city or house divided against itself shall not stand'. From the gospel of Matthew.' Miller paused after he made this quote. There was complete silence among the little assembly. 'I expect nothing but complete loyalty from you. If any of you feel it is too much to ask then I want you to leave my employ now. Go downtown to the bank and draw what wages are due. What goes on in this house is private. Anyone who invades this privacy must be ousted immediately.

'A young woman of this household aided and abetted a group of ruffians who came here in my absence. I've had to discipline her. I went light on her punishment for she is young and perhaps does not yet know the meaning of loyalty. In future, any infringements of this nature will be punished more severely. When I say severely I mean instant dismissal and a term in jail.' Miller glared round at the assembled staff. No one dared meet his eyes. 'Loyalty means reporting any disloyal behaviour on the part of your fellow members in this household. Any information brought to me in this way will be treated in the strictest confidence. I will say no more on this subject. You all know what is expected of you.'

Their heads hung low. There was complete silence in the big room.

'Tom, I want you to ride out to the old Corley place. Tell the men out there to come in and see me.'

Abruptly, Miller turned and stalked from the room. Tom arose and went after him. It was a long time before anyone in the big kitchen dared move.

24

Joe lay just inside the cave mouth and watched the valley stretching out before him. While he did sentry duty the ex carpenter idly speculated on the various trees, wondering to what use he could put such good growing wood. His carpentry days seemed in another life, as were the wife and baby he had left back East.

The sun was dipping below the far wall of the valley and tinged the rim with a blood-red light. Shadows grew long and blurred in the valley bottom. Joe tensed as he spotted movement below.

A body of horsemen emerged from the tree line and rode slowly, studying the area as they progressed. Eventually the leading horseman raised his arm and the cavalcade came to a halt. Even though Joe was far above the horsemen he held his breath as if afraid the men could hear his breathing. He feared they had found some sign that indicated to them where the fugitives had hidden.

Some sort of discussion was going on. Joe eased the shotgun forward. If the posse came up the trail seeking them out, the cave was an easy place to defend. Only one man at a time could ascend the narrow track. The defenders could hold out for days. Food would be a problem though. Joe and companions could be starved out. Frank was the main worry. As it was, it was touch and go if the wounded man would survive in such primitive conditions. As he pondered all this he saw with some apprehension the men of the posse were dismounting.

'Damn, they've spotted our sign.'

He considered alerting his companions but decided to wait until the members of the posse began the ascent up to the cave. There was a lot of milling about as the posse dismounted.

Suddenly the men began walking back towards the trees.

Horses were tethered there and, to his surprise, men began unbuckling saddles. Others began to gather wood and Joe realized the posse was establishing a camp. A fire was started and men gathered round. Joe watched the activity as utensils were unpacked and food prepared.

'Goddamn it, they're gonna keep us bottled up here and attack in the morning.'

He kept watch a while longer till he was sure that no immediate foray was being planned then he got to his feet and walked inside to his companions.

Butch had spread a blanket and was busy cleaning the weapons they had used in their breakout from the Miller mansion. Jessica sat close to Frank and was bathing the old man's face. It was pinched and drawn.

'The posse's down in the valley. They seem intent on camping for the night. My guess is, they'll wait till morning and come for us then.'

'What's to stop them attacking tonight?' Butch asked.

'They might,' Joe agreed. 'Somehow I don't think so.'

'Even so, we gotta keep watch through the night. We'll havta take it in turns.'

'I agree. Seeing as I started I'll take first watch. How's Frank?' he asked Jessica.

'He's still out. Doesn't look too good. He really needs a doctor.'

The big man reached over and patted the girl's hand. 'Don't you fret. You're doing your best. I'm sorry you're stuck in the middle of this.'

She smiled at him wearily. 'You saved my life back there by rescuing me from that big house.'

Joe rose from the fire and walked back to his guard duty. Butch looked up from his gun cleaning.

'Tell me everything what happened back at that place,' he said to the girl. 'Why do you think they grabbed you?'

So she told him about overhearing the men in the livery. 'They said as I was a runaway and my ma and pa wanted me back. Then Mr Miller said the same thing. I recalled that Frank said as I was a witness to murder.' She was silent while they both mulled this over. 'One thing else I learned while I was there. Ruth, the girl as helped me, told me Mrs Miller went off with some banker fella. When she returned she was with those men we think did all those killings. Funny thing they took her along with them.'

'Beats me.'

They were silent then, mulling over the events of the last few days.

* * *

Butch awoke with an uneasy feeling. He had been dreaming he was back at his old job of herding cows. Now he looked about him with a sleepy haze fogging his senses.

'Jeepers, I musta fell asleep.'

He blinked in the darkness and looked around him. The scrape of a boot heel came again.

'Joe,' he whispered, 'is that you?'

He had taken over from Joe on lookout duty late into the night. They had decided to spare Jessica her turn as she had been looking after Frank with such diligence. He groped for his rifle, not finding it in the dark.

They came into the cave at a rush. Butch had been lying propped against the wall of the cave. Not seeing him in the dark the first man tripped over his outstretched legs. There was a muffled curse.

Butch's hand at last closed over the rifle stock. He swung hard, still not able to see what he was lashing out at. There was a yell as the rifle jarred in his hand against something solid. A gun boomed from the cave mouth just a few feet from Butch.

The bullet smacked into the rock face beside him and ricocheted inside. He heard the whine as it passed overhead. By now he had his rifle aimed at the muzzle flash and he pulled the trigger. The heavier boom of the rifle echoed loudly inside the cave. There was another cry in the night and the shadowy figure in the entrance disappeared.

This heralded a flurry of shots and bullets rained inside striking against the rock face and ricocheting like angry hornets in the dark. Butch flung himself prone and poked his rifle outside. He let off a few shots. His actions only seemed to increase the number of shots from the attackers. He felt a hand on his ankle and rolled around to meet this new danger.

'It's me, dang you!' Joe yelled, seeing his partner swing his rifle towards him.

The big man wriggled forward till he was beside Butch. Angling his shotgun in the direction of the path he let fly with one barrel. The intensity of the shooting from outside slackened off somewhat. Joe waited a moment and changed the angle of his deadly weapon. His second shot brought a scream and the firing ceased abruptly. There was the clatter of boots as the attackers fled back down the path. They heard someone cry out as he tripped and tumbled down the path. Joe quickly reloaded.

'Butch, you all right?'

'Sure, Joe, just a bit shaken. There should be one of them inside here. I clouted him with my rifle.' As if to confirm his statement someone groaned. 'Keep a eye while I find out who this fella is.'

'Help me . . . I'm shot. Is that you, Tim?'

'No it ain't Tim,' Butch answered. 'Where you hit?'

'Oh, Gawd, it hurts so. Help me . . . '

Butch was kneeling beside the wounded man. As he leant over he heard the distinct click of a hammer coming back.

'Shit!'

He rolled to one side and kicked out viciously with his feet. The man's revolver went off and the flash blinded the cowboy as he frantically tried to bring his own rifle to bear. Then Butch went deaf as the shotgun went off behind him. He felt the heat of the blast as the densely packed shot gusted past him. There was the sickly thud of lead smashing into flesh and Butch felt a wetness splatter over his face and clothing.

'Goddamn it! Goddamn it to hell!' he yelled, as he pawed frantically at his face.

There was no way to see in the dark but he guessed the man's head was splattered over the cave as well as spurting over him. He could smell the blood with the cordite mixed in.

'Butch, Butch, you OK?'

'Goddamn you to hell, Joe Peters! Why'd you havta do that?' Butch yelled. 'I had him covered.'

But Butch knew he had come near to falling for the man's trick. Only for his partner's quick actions it could well have been him lying dead now on the floor of the cave instead of the intruder.

'Don't do that again!' he bellowed, the fright of the near miss making him lash out at Joe.

'All right then!' Joe found himself yelling back. The near miss had frightened him as well as his partner. 'Next time I'll let them blast out what little brains you got in that thick skull of yours.'

'Keep a lookout,' Butch snarled. 'They might wanna rush us again.'

'I suppose you fell asleep,' Joe retorted, turning back to the cave entrance and peering cautiously outside.

Nothing moved in the darkness. Below he could see the camp-fire blazing as someone threw fresh fuel into it. He could hear Butch cursing under his breath as he moved up beside him.

'I guess I made a mess of the fella back there,' Joe said after a long silence.

'I guess,' came the reply.

'This place stinks of blood.'

It was too dark for Joe to see the look the cowboy threw at him.

25

The men filed into the house and Geraint ushered them down the corridor. They were the men who had been brought in from the old Corley place. They were the very same men who had stained the walls of Empire Fastness Way Station with blood.

Jabez was the mean-looking elder of the group. Behind him came Marcus, bearded with a ponytail; Charlie, the young blond one, who had sparked up to the half-breed girl at the way station; Dave, tall, youthful, moving with an easy grace. And last came Eli, mean and brooding. All men with cruel natures and a grudge against the world.

Crossed gunbelts held Navy Colts. Each possessed a razor-sharp sheath knife. They made a formidable gang of villains. The sort of men that inclined ordinary folk to go indoors and cower till the wolves had moved on.

'That'll be all, Geraint. I'll call you when I need you.'

The big man backed out of the room. Once the door closed behind him the men dispersed around the room perching on chairs and couches. They looked indolent and at ease as they settled.

Granville Miller grabbed up a carved rosewood box and dispensed fat cigars to his visitors. He returned to his large desk of polished mahogany and replaced the cigar box.

'Drink anyone?' Without waiting for a reply he poured generous measures of bourbon from a decanter. 'Help yourselves,' he invited, indicating the brimming tumblers.

There was a general shift of bodies as the gang came forward and grabbed the drinks. Gradually the room settled down as the men lit up and sipped their bourbon. Miller fixed his eyes on the old man, Jabez.

'Did you stop at a farm on the way back from that way station?'

Jabez stared back evenly at Miller. 'What if we did?'

'Seems like someone rode into that farm and murdered the couple as owned it. Problem is there was a witness. Their daughter saw the whole thing and can identify the killers.'

There was movement around the room as the group took in this information.

'Three fellas rode in yesterday with that girl. They were making enquiries about you. They reckon they tracked you from Empire Fastness Way Station. I had them penned up in the jail but they bust loose. Sheriff's posse is out there now searching for them. I ain't got much faith in that bunch of dim-wits. It would take someone with your kinda skills for this job. Those fellas could make an awful lot of trouble for us. They need to be taken care of — permanently — along with the girl.'

'That shouldn't be a problem. What direction did they go?'

'Out towards the buttes past the

mine workings. The posse already had a run in with them. They sent back three wounded men this morning — said they had those fellas holed up in some caves. They can't get at them. Sheriff wants me to send him food and more men. They reckon to starve them out.'

'Mr Miller, we'll take care of it,' Jabez intoned. He tossed off the last of the bourbon and stood. There was a scrambling of boots as his men did likewise.

'How's my wife bearing up?' Miller had stood up also.

'She sends you a message. Says as she's sorry she ran off with that banker man and wants to come back home.'

'What do you think, Jabez?' Miller leaned forward, his hands resting on the large wooden desk. 'Think she's truly contrite?'

'Like I told you afore, when we caught up with her on that stage we gutted that fella she ran away with like you would a fish. She didn't take much to that and fainted on us. We had to wait for her to come around afore completing the son-abitch's initiation of blood. She's had time to reflect on that.' The mean-looking older man drew hard on the cigar, sucking in his cheeks so he looked more like a walking skull than ever. 'I guess she's learnt her lesson.'

'What about the girl you brought along with her?'

'Ah, that's a different skillet of beans.' The outlaw leader blew a plume of smoke. 'I fear she is much abused. Your wife pleads for her but my boys don't take much heed.'

'OK Jabez, when all this is over you can send Mrs Miller back home. What you do with the girl is your business.'

The men stalked from the room trailing cigar smoke and taking with them a sense of something malevolent.

★ ★ ★

'Joe.'

The big man turned as he heard Jessica call his name. Leaving Butch to

218

keep watch he went back down the cave.

'What is it?'

'It's Frank, he looks real bad. I don't know much about these things but I'm afraid for him.'

Joe knelt beside the old man. Instead of his usual dark suntan Frank looked so pale he was almost luminous. Joe felt his neck for a pulse and located a feeble indication of life.

'He needs a doctor, otherwise he'll never last.' Joe bent his head in an attitude of despair. 'I'd better consult with Butch.'

Back at the entrance to the cave Joe squatted down beside Butch.

'What is it?'

'Frank ain't gonna survive without a doctor.'

'Poor old boy, what we gonna do?'

'Butch, we gotta give ourselves up. It's the only way we gonna get help for Frank.'

Both men were silent as they gazed down at the posse. A huge fire had been built up. Men sat around smoking and drinking coffee.

'They'll stay there forever till we give up. They can send back to town for fresh men and supplies.'

As if to confirm this a bunch of riders could be seen coming out of the trees and heading towards the camp. There were five men in the group. None of them dismounted when they reached the camp. It was obvious there was some debate going on.

'You know they'll hang us, Joe.'

Joe looked down at his big capable hands, hands that were more used to handling saws and planes than the killing tools he had been forced to use ever since that fateful card game in Hinkly when he had accidentally slain the card sharp.

'You think I don't know that.'

'What about Jessica? That Miller fella will want her killed as well to shut her from blabbing about him. She figures he's somehow mixed up with those killers as murdered her ma and pa.'

They were silent for a moment as they thought out the consequences of handing themselves over to the posse.

'If'n we leave her up here in the cave — pretend she weren't with us, maybe she could sneak away when we gone.'

'You know they could be riled up enough to lynch us outta hand.'

'We gotta take that chance. It's that or Frank is gonna die for sure.'

The two men stared into each other's eyes probing for a sign of weakness. On sudden impulse they reached towards each other and grasped hands.

'It's been good knowing you, Butch.'

'Joe, for a dude from back East, I reckon you'll do to ride the trail with.'

Which was high praise indeed from the cowboy.

26

Using the blanket as a makeshift stretcher the two friends shuffled down the precarious path. At the bottom of the hill an arsenal of guns were trained on the stretcher-bearers.

'Hell,' muttered Butch, 'if those galoots start shooting there won't be enough of us left for to gather up for a decent burial.'

'Well, at least it'll be quick. Not like poor Frank here.'

Under the ominous threat of the guns they continued their descent. Using a white flag made from one of the cloths filched from Miller's kitchen, they had negotiated a deal with the posse. They had left their weapons in the cave with Jessica. She had strict instructions from the two wanted men to keep herself hidden.

'We'll tell them you stayed behind in

Coventree with some friends. They ain't to know any difference. But keep a sharp lookout. If anybody starts up towards the cave to look for you, start shooting. We know you can fire a rifle. Miller and his owlhoot friends wants you dead. As soon as the coast is clear you light outta here. Go to the nearest big town and tell your story to the authorities there. With a bit of luck you might even be in time to save our necks.'

'What you saying? You think they'll hang you?'

'Nah, it's just a way of speaking. They'll sling us in jail and there'll havta be some sorta trial. In the meantime it'll be your job to keep safe and bring the cavalry to our rescue.'

It had taken all the persuasive powers of both Joe and Butch to coerce the young girl into complying with their instructions. She had finally agreed to do as they wanted.

When they left, carrying Frank, she had lain flat inside the cave with her rifle in her hands and the men's discarded weapons lined up beside her. Inching forward she peered down at the armed reception committee awaiting the arrival of the two men and their wounded companion.

It was no easy task navigating the path while holding the ends of the blanket laden with the dead weight of the badly wounded Frank, but at last the two friends arrived at the bottom.

'Don't make any sudden moves and keep hold of that blanket.' The sheriff was a tall spare man with a drooping moustache. Keeping his carbine on the fugitives he moved closer and looked down at the man in the blanket. 'Hmm . . . he does look in a bad way. OK, bring him over here to the fire. We got a wagon headed out this way bringing supplies for us we can use to take your friend to town.'

A gaunt oldster with hard, staring eyes stepped forward. He held a Colt .44 casually pointed at the captives. 'That's all right, Sheriff, we'll take over now. You take your men on back to town. You done enough.'

'What the hell you mean? These are my prisoners and I'll take charge of them.'

Those mean eyes turned fully on the lawman. The sheriff flinched as he tried to meet the cold-eyed stare.

'Sheriff, the last time you had these men behind bars they walked. I aim to see they get safe to jail. They won't escape from me.'

'Damn you,' the sheriff blustered. 'I'm in charge here.'

To the lawman's discomfiture the barrel of the big Colt turned in his direction.

'Mister Miller ain't going to be too pleased if'n these fellas escape justice for a second time. He specifically asked me to personally escort the prisoners to town to stand trial.'

For a second only the sheriff glared his displeasure, but he could not hold out against those fixed cold eyes. 'It ain't right,' he mumbled. 'I'm the official law around here. It's my responsibility . . . '

A youngster moved up to the sheriff. He took out a large Bowie and not saying anything he began to pick at the lawman's shirt with the point.

'What the hell . . . ' The sheriff stepped back from that deadly looking blade.

The youngster smiled at the sheriff. He was shorter than the lawman. As if to make up for his stunted height he had broad powerful shoulders. 'I never stuck no lawman afore,' he said affably. 'Stuck me hogs and fellas as I had argument with, but no lawmen.'

The sheriff got an impression he was dealing with someone deranged. 'This is most irregular,' he spluttered. 'You men have no authority.'

'Just you ride into town and tell Mr Miller he has no authority to appoint us fellas to bring in these owlhoots. If'n he takes your side we'll gladly hand them over. Now you and your deputies ride outta here.'

The sheriff glared round him. And suddenly he noticed the five men who had ridden in to join the posse were spread around so they had every one of the sheriff's men under a gun.

'We're taking these men into jail, Sheriff.' As he spoke, the gaunt man was alternately looking down at his Colt and then up at the sheriff 'One way or another we're taking these men.'

There was no mistaking the menace in the man's eyes and voice. The sheriff quailed before him.

'I . . . I'll ride in and ask Mr Miller myself. It don't seem right.'

'That's right, Sheriff, you just do that.'

While this bizarre exchange was going on Butch and Joe gently lowered the blanket with the wounded Frank. The movement drew everyone's attention back to them and a forest of gun barrels once more moved to cover them.

'Marcus, Dave, cover these two,' rasped out Jabez.

The tall youngster and the one with the ponytail dangling from under his hat moved up towards Joe and Butch.

'What about Frank here?' Joe asked 'He's the reason we come down. He needs a doctor urgent.'

'Shuddup!'

As he spoke Dave lashed out with his Colt taking Joe across the side of the head. The big man was not expecting the attack and staggered back.

'Damn you!' Joe yelled.

He launched himself at his attacker but a sudden shot from Dave's gun hit him in the arm and knocked him sideways. Joe swayed somewhat as he stared at the youngster. He grabbed at his wounded arm and a spasm of pain crossed his face.

Butch had tensed ready to come to Joe's aid but the unexpected shot brought a halt to any action on his part. With so many guns trained on them they stood no chance if they attacked such a large bunch of armed men.

'You see, Sheriff, what desperadoes

we have caught here,' Jabez drawled. 'Now you just ride on into town and tell Mr Miller we're bringing these fellas in.'

'I . . . I guess so,' the sheriff said shakily. 'Come on, fellas.'

As the sheriff and his posse readied themselves to ride back to town Butch was examining the men who were to take charge of the prisoners. The cowboy was not impressed with what he saw. The gaunt older man had an aura of menace about him while his sidekicks looked every bit as dangerous.

'What about Frank?' Butch ventured keeping a wary eye on Dave as he spoke.

'Don't you worry he'll be taken care of,' the sheriff assured Butch. 'There's a wagon on the way from town. We'll more'n likely meet it on the way in. It'll take your friend to town and the sawbones will take care of him.'

'Adios, Sheriff,' Jabez called pointedly.

Butch watched the posse ride away.

He had an uneasy feeling about all this. The attitude and behaviour of the men left behind was not that of a lawfully appointed posse but more reminiscent of a bunch of hardcases. He was not reassured when the gaunt old man turned and stared at him out of fish-cold eyes.

'Now we can take care of these dudes.'

27

'Damn you, my arm's bleeding.'

Butch looked at his friend. The big man was holding his wounded arm and blood could be seen oozing between his fingers.

'Is that a fact?' Dave answered. 'Maybe I should put one in the other arm to balance you up.'

'Get them over to the trees,' growled Jabez.

'What about Frank?' Butch gestured towards the wounded man lying where they had deposited him. 'You said you'd take care of him.'

'You and your friend bring him with you. We'll take care of him all right.'

Butch and Joe took up the ends of the blanket. In spite of the wound in his arm Joe took his share of the burden. With drawn guns their captors ushered them towards the camp-fire. Gently the two friends laid the wounded man beside the fire.

'Throw some more wood on that there fire,' the leader of the group ordered Butch.

A large pile of branches had been gathered in by the posse — evidence of their determination to wait out the fugitives.

'OK git the rope, Marcus.'

The dark youngster with the ponytail walked to the tethered horses and walked back grinning as he carried the rope. He strode to the trees and looked up. Then he slung the rope. It was a good throw and looped over a thick branch. Butch turned a puzzled look towards Joe. The big man was looking with the same perplexed expression on his face.

'Git him up there!'

The purpose of the rope became all too clear as Marcus walked to the fire. He and Dave bent and without ceremony grabbed Frank by the legs and began dragging the wounded man towards the rope.

'No,' screamed Butch, and began running forward. In his hand was a stout piece of firewood. 'Damn you no!'

The shot blasted out. Butch felt something sting his ear and then he stumbled as a foot reached out and tripped him. He didn't see the gun barrel that slashed across his head. His face was pushed into the dirt and a boot in the back of his head held him there.

'Heave ho!' someone shouted.

The pressure of the boot holding him down was released and Butch raised his head and groaned. He wanted to close his eyes but he could not take his gaze from that slowly twisting, swinging figure suspended from the neck by the rope.

'No,' he whispered. 'Frank ... no ... '

But the body of the old man continued to swing beneath the tree in slow motion. Butch could hear a struggle and Joe crashed down beside him. But Butch could not take his eyes from the dreadful sight of the old man hanging from the tree.

Slowly the suspended body twisted around and they saw the face. The eyes had opened, as had the mouth. Frank's lips writhed and twisted in a horrible parody of speech. His tongue protruded and his eyeballs bulged as the last vestige of life was throttled from him. Feebly the legs twitched but even that eventually ceased.

The body of their friend swayed gently back and forth with hypnotic motion. Butch buried his aching head in the dirt once more in an attempt to blot out the ghastly sight.

Rough hands grabbed the two prisoners and turned them over so they lay helpless on their backs, staring up at a circle of guns.

'How did you like the first act of our little show?' cackled the gaunt old man. 'The second act requires audience participation.'

They looked up into a face from hell.

The old man was grinning down at them with his skull-like features. In his hand was a burning brand he had plucked from the fire.

'That wound needs some attention,' the hellhound continued. 'Let me cauterize it.'

With a sudden movement the old fiend bent forward and pushed the end of blazing branch into Joe's wounded arm. It was so unexpected and brutally painful the big man screamed out in sudden agony.

'Damn you to hell!'

Joe twisted about as the pain in his wound intensified with the brutal treatment. Butch was trying to rise when a boot kicked him in the head. His ear had been bleeding from the earlier bullet that had been intended for his head. The boot smashed into the injury, intensifying the pain.

'Aaahhh!'

The agony in his head momentarily disabled the cowboy. He clapped both hands to his injury. Blood was running down his neck and inside his shirt. His hands were slippery with the crimson flood pouring from the damaged ear.

'Now, fellas, we been easy on you so far. We want some answers. If you don't answer promptly we burn you or cut you, or if you're real stubborn, then we hang you up there beside your partner.'

'Go to hell,' Butch yelled.

An agonizing flame of agony lanced through him as one of the men kicked him viciously between his legs. He opened his eyes and through tears of pain saw the man called Dave grinning down at him. With a sudden awful realization Butch guessed at the identity of these sadistic men.

'You're them!' he gasped. 'You're the butchers from Empire Fastness Way Station.'

'OK, fella.' The skull-like face of the old man was looming over him, the smouldering branch still his hand. 'That's a start. How did you find us?'

Butch stared into those cold fish eyes and shuddered. Not one who had ever been afraid of anything in his life, he saw the face of evil and a stab of fear dug deep into his bowels. The memory of the bloody butchery back at the way station surfaced in his mind and he knew with sudden certainty that Joe and he were not meant to survive this ordeal.

'There were two lawmen at the way station. Were they friends of yours?'

Slowly Butch nodded. The movement hurt his head where he had been hit with the gun barrel. His ear ached but not as much as his balls where he had been kicked.

'Yes,' he mumbled, 'we were the backup.'

'Goddamn it, speak up.' The face bent closer.

Butch raised his hands as if to ward off the threat the old man posed. The burning brand edged closer and closer to the cowboy's face. He could feel the heat from the blaze and a few hot splinters fell onto his forehead.

'Please, mister,' he pleaded, 'don't hurt us any more. I'll tell you everything.'

28

With a suddenness that took the old man by surprise Butch's hand closed over the fist holding the torch. With brutal strength he rammed the smouldering end into that grinning skull. At the same time his other hand gripped the old man's waistcoat and he jerked him close.

The man was screaming as the hot brand burned his eyes. He was thrashing about on top of Butch. The cowboy loosened his grip and was groping for a holster. At the same time he kept twisting the burning stick into the man's face. His hand closed over a gun butt. Butch jerked and the gun was free. He saw the big man Dave in front of him raising his gun. Butch shot him in the gut.

The big bandit gasped and staggered back. He had been angling for a shot at the cowboy but couldn't get a clear aim because of the old man lying on top. With a sudden groan he sank to the ground, clutching at his midriff.

Butch relinquished his hold on the burning faggot and it fell into the dirt. He grabbed the blinded man and held him close, making an effective shield against the bullets of his companions. The man was screaming and pawing at his damaged eyes.

Butch swivelled the Colt aiming at the shadowy figures around him. He could not make out details of the men he was shooting at but he reasoned anyone standing was an enemy. When last he had seen his partner he was on the ground writhing in agony as the old man applied the burning brand to his wound.

Ponytail fired at Butch but aimed wide for fear of hitting the old man struggling frantically to free himself from Butch's grip.

The gunmen were ignoring Joe and concentrating their efforts on finishing

Butch and rescuing their leader. From his prone position on the dirt, the big man launched a kick at Charlie, the stocky, blond gunman. As the man went down, Joe, ignoring the pain in his wounded arm, was on the outlaw like a cat springing on an rat.

For a moment he saw stars as Charlie's pistol cracked into his skull. Then Joe rammed his forehead into the outlaw's face. The unexpected blow momentarily stunned the outlaw. But he was brutally strong and, recovering quickly, he swung once more with his weapon. The heavy revolver crashed into Joe's head once again.

Fighting against the pain the big man reached out with his good arm and grabbed the hand holding the weapon. For a few moments the two men struggled for possession of the gun. They were both strong men. Joe was at a disadvantage because of his disabled arm, but he knew he was fighting for his life.

He was bitterly angry also. He had

just seen his friend callously strangled on the end of a rope. He wanted revenge for that murder. All reason left him. Ignoring the pain in his injured arm he rammed his fist into the youngster's face. Blood was pouring from his busted nose where Joe had already butted him.

Joe's big meaty fist smashed into the injury and the nose was further crushed. More blood poured out of the damaged cartilage. The outlaw screamed out in rage. He struggled madly beneath Joe as he tried to throw the big man from him. Joe held grimly to the gun with his uninjured hand and punched again and again at the upturned face now crimson with blood.

Somewhere on one side Butch was also fighting for his life. He did not know if he had managed to hit anyone with the shots from the purloined revolver. Then his hammer clicked on an empty chamber.

'Damn!' he swore. The screaming of the blinded man he was hugging close was deafening him. Suddenly a figure loomed over him and he saw the face of the youngster with the ponytail glaring down at him. The face was twisted with hate as the outlaw stared down at the trapped cowboy. In his hand he was holding a revolver.

'Die, you bastard!' the twisted face screamed.

He was so close spittle from his distorted mouth splashed on to the cowboy lying trapped beneath the leader of the outlaws. The muzzle of the gun was rammed against Butch's forehead. There was a sudden thud of lead striking bone and for one instant Butch thought he was dead. The gun slid along the side of the cowboy's head and he watched in bewilderment as the gunman's head disintegrated and blood and brains splashed on to his upturned face.

'Goddamn, am I dead or what?'

Butch now had two bodies to contend with. One was moaning and pawing at burned-out eyes and the other was dribbling red mush from a shattered skull.

Butch went a little crazy then. Now it was he thrashing around in a frenzy as he tried to break away from the horrors pinning him to the dirt.

The blinded leader rolled away and Butch was able to push the outlaw with the shattered head to one side. He sat up, his head reeling. A scene of confusion greeted him as he tried to make sense of the bodies lying around the camp-fire.

As an afterthought, he grabbed for the gun in the hand of the dead man lying beside him with his head blown apart. He heard the grunts and curses of a tussle going on behind him. He turned and saw his partner in a death struggle with the powerfully built young blond thug.

Blood was running down Joe's arm and pooling on the ground as he used that injured arm to strangle the youngster beneath him. The outlaw's face was covered with blood also and his mouth gaped wide as Joe held relentlessly to his grip on the outlaw's throat. A discarded gun lay in the dirt beside them.

Butch began to crawl towards the struggling pair. He was on his hands and knees, not sure if he could stand. His head was a dull ball of agony. The pain in his groin where Dave had kicked him worsened with each movement he made. He groaned as the anguish of his tortured body protested but kept moving towards the violent struggle between the two powerful combatants.

It was over before he reached them. The outlaw's struggles grew feeble and his grip on Joe's fingers slackened. There was a hideous grunt deep inside his throat. Joe never slackened his stranglehold. Slowly the outlaw's hands fell to his sides and his struggles ceased.

Joe was still maintaining that death grip when he felt a hand on his arm. He glanced round thinking he had another attacker to contend with. A face encrusted with blood and what looked like the bits of a dead animal was peering at him. The mouth on the bloody face opened and a voice he knew from somewhere croaked, 'Joe, you can let go now. That fella's done for.'

Slowly Joe relaxed and tried to push himself from the body of the man he had just strangled. His wounded arm gave way and with a grunt he sagged to the dirt. He lay on his back and heaved great breaths. The sky never looked so beautiful. Then he was jerked out of his reverie by the crack of a rifle followed by the distinct zing of a bullet passing close overhead.

29

'Goddamn, I thought they were all down,' Butch yelled.

He still held the gun he had grabbed when the outlaw had his brains blown apart. More shots were buzzing around them as they twisted about to face this new threat. A bizarre sight met their eyes.

Swaying drunkenly before them was the leader of the bandits. His blistered and blackened face was staring sightlessly towards them. In his hands he held a rifle that he was pointing in their direction and spacing his shots one by one at them. He stopped firing and cocked his head to one side, standing motionless like a smoke-blackened gargoyle listening for the sounds that would indicate where his enemies were.

The two battered men lay motionless, frozen in horror at the sight of this dangerous creature. Injured and blinded he was as deadly as a cornered animal.

'Damn you,' the blind head screamed. 'I know you're there. Charlie, Dave, where are you?' The grotesque, blackened face was turning from side to side questing for sign. 'Eli, Marcus . . . '

The rifle fired again. Joe and Butch lay motionless, afraid to move — afraid to draw the deadly attention of that blind but dangerous creature seeking them out. Joe saw the gun in his companion's hand.

'Shoot him,' he whispered.

That tiny sound was enough for the old man. The rifle spouted flame and this time the bullet ploughed into the dead man lying between them. Butch knew it was only a matter of time before one of those deadly missiles hit him or his partner. He aimed at the old man's chest and pulled the trigger. The sightless head came up with the shock of the impact. In spite of being hit, the gunman fired again, Butch shot another bullet and the old man stepped back under the impact. He still did not go down.

'Damn you,' the blind gargoyle screamed defiantly, and fired again towards the sound of the revolver.

Butch shot again and again, each bullet hitting the old man and jerking him back a step at a time. The hammer clicked on an empty shell. The cowboy looked round desperately for another weapon. The rifle fire ceased. He glanced back towards the blinded killer.

The man was sitting on the dirt. His body swayed from side to side. The rifle was pointing towards the ground. The blind man tried to bring it up level again but his strength was draining away with the terrible wounds he had taken. Slowly he keeled over on his side — even as he died his blackened skull was kept turned towards his foes.

The two friends lay on their backs, bleeding into the dirt.

'Joe, how are you?'

'I felt better.' There was a groan as Joe tried to sit up favouring his wounded arm. 'How are you?'

'Pretty done in.' Butch sat up — his head spinning with the movement.

They gazed round the battlefield. The bodies of the outlaw gang were strewn around in a circle.

'Joe.' Someone was calling. 'Butch.'

Down the cliff path came Jessica holding her rifle as she descended.

'Jessica,' they called out together. 'It's OK, we're safe.'

Wearily they climbed to their feet. Jessica ran across the last few yards. She hugged first Butch and then Joe.

'I . . . I thought you were goners.'

Butch was looking quizzically at the rifle the girl was carrying. 'It was you. You shot that *hombre*.'

'Oh, Butch, I saw him kneeling there pointing his gun. I was afraid to shoot for fear of hitting any of you. But I knew if I didn't make it he woulda killed you.'

'Jessica, you saved my life!'

'I saw what they done to Frank. I was so scared.' She was shaking and the tears came flooding down her cheeks.

Joe stepped forward and wrapped his good arm around the weeping girl. 'We're safe now, girl. And you done your bit to keep us safe.'

The sound of rumbling wheels intruded on the quiet of the morning. They looked towards the entrance to the valley. Into sight lumbered a wagon. When the driver saw them standing there he waved and called out a greeting. The trio stood there waiting, unsure of what this new development heralded.

The wagon drew up near them and the driver, a stringy looking fellow with bony hands and wrists sat gazing at the bodies strewn around the campsite.

'Hell, I bin through Bull Run and Gettysburg, but I never seed anything like this. You fellas bin fightin' a war up here?'

'Seems like it,' Butch answered.

He was unaware of his bizarre appearance. His face was encrusted with blood and bits of brain that had splattered over him when Jessica shot the bandit about to kill him.

'I'm supposed to pick up a wounded man. Met the sheriff on the way up. Told me where to come. You got some prisoners to bring back also?' Suddenly he spotted the body hanging from the tree. 'Goddamn it, you fellas bin hangin' the prisoners already?'

Joe released Jessica and waved his good arm around the camp. 'It were these fellas as started the hanging. We were to be next.'

The groan when it came took them all by surprise. Butch snatched the rifle from Jessica. After experiencing the toughness of the bandit leader he did not want to face another of the gang no matter how badly wounded he might be. Joe was moving across the campsite searching for the person who had made the distress sound.

'Here,' he called.

It was Dave, the first man Butch had shot while trapped beneath the blinded leader. He was curled on his side holding his stomach. Blood soaked the front of his shirt.

'Help me,' he moaned.

Joe knelt beside the wounded man. 'Hang on there, fella, we got a wagon here to take you to town. The sawbones will take care of you.'

'Jeez, Joe, you think we gonna help this trash after what they did to Frank?'

Joe turned round and stared at his companions. 'Butch, what the hell you talking about! That'll make us just as bad as them. We ain't killers by choice.'

Joe frowned as he saw the cowboy winking at him.

'Maybe if he tells us what happened at Empire Fastness Way Station and why they come out here to kill us we might just help him.'

Joe turned back to the wounded man. 'You hear that, fella? You ready to confess?'

'Help me; I don't know nothing.'

'We'll cut down Frank and string this galoot up in his place.'

'No, no . . . I'll tell you everything

when you get me to the sawbones.'

'Get that rope!' Butch snarled. 'He ain't gonna tell us nothing.'

He reached down and grabbed the man's collar and started to haul him towards the trees.

'Hang on there, fella,' the wagon driver protested. 'I don't wanna be no party to no hangin'.'

'Look the other way, then!' Butch growled.

'Please don't ... I'll tell you everything.'

'What happened at Empire Fastness Way Station?'

'Miller's wife ran off with a fella as wanted to set up a bank in Brimingdam. He had a lotta money with him on the coach. Miller told us where to go. We were to kill the banker and bring back Miller's wife and the money. I had nothing to do with the killings. I just stood lookout. I thought it was gonna be robbery. I didn't want no part in the killings.'

Butch grabbed the outlaw by his

shirtfront. 'There was another female — a young girl. What happened to the girl?'

'Charlie took a fancy to her. He wanted her for himself. She's back at the cabin with Mrs Miller.'

'Hang on there,' the wagon driver interjected. 'You fellas talkin' about Mr Miller what owns about all of Coventree?'

'The very one, fella. He sent these killers out to finish us off so as we wouldn't testify against him.'

'Well, I'll be danged! Mr Self-Righteous Miller.' The driver pushed his hat to the back of his head. 'Well, I'll be danged!'

30

They loaded the bodies into the wagon. Under protest the wounded outlaw was put inside with his dead buddies.

'Just be thankful, fella, we aren't like your pards. Otherwise you'd be hanging from that cottonwood just as you hanged our friend.'

'We can't carry Frank into Coventree in the back of that meat wagon. Them coyotes ain't fit to ride in the same vehicle.'

It was Butch who suggested they bury their old friend in the valley. 'He was a man as roamed free. He wouldn't have wanted to be buried in no town cemetery. Surely he would be happier lying out here in this peaceful valley where he met his end.'

There was a feeling of great loss among the three friends as they stood over the grave mound.

'Can anyone say a few words?'

Each looked hopefully at the other. Finally it was Joe who took it upon himself to speak the funeral oration.

'Frank, old-timer, you were a true friend. Somehow I feel you grabbed the sticky end of the spoon when you joined up with Butch and me. Well, old-timer, you're at rest now. We'll miss you, Frank. Rest in peace.'

It was a sober party that rode away from that place of death. The meat wagon led the way followed by Joe cradling his arm in a sling put there on the insistence of Jessica.

The ex-carpenter was reflecting on the path that had led him to this place and the bloodletting that seemed to dog him since he had accidentally killed the card sharp back in Hinkly.

'Once the killing starts it seems to take on a life of its own,' he muttered.

Behind him, rode Jessica huddled low in her saddle, her young spirits weighed down by the brutal events of the last few days. She had seen her parents slaughtered by the brutal gang of killers. The banker Miller had imprisoned her in his big house. Back in the valley she had buried a man she considered a friend. She had also killed her first man back there. She was the one most thankful to be leaving that valley of death behind.

Butch came last in the procession. The cowboy had tried to wash clean the blood and debris of the killings back in the valley. His clothes still bore the traces of blood and brains that had splattered him during their fight for survival in that fateful place.

He had set out on this quest because he had promised a dying man he would rescue his sister. Much blood had been spilt that terrible day at the way station. Now the blood-crazed killers had paid the price for their crimes. They lay together in death as they had been in life within the wagon taking them to Coventree for burial.

' 'Vengeance is mine, saith the Lord',' he muttered.

It only left the task of locating the cabin Dave had told them about and freeing the young girl and Mrs Miller.

'Miller,' he muttered. 'Granville Aloysius Garrett Miller,' he repeated the name as he remembered the banker had said it. 'A grand name. It should look good on his tombstone.'

Well, his job was almost done. The law would take care of Miller. He had carried out his promise to the dying man back at the way station.

'We have waded through much blood to get to this day. I am tired of killing. I wanna hang up my guns for good and all. I'll get me a little spread — run a few cows,' he muttered.

Then he was minded of the ten-year sentence hanging over him and he knew he could not easily realize his dream of the quiet life.

It was gone noon when they rode into Coventree. The laden wagon braked in front of the sheriff's office. The sheriff came on to the boardwalk when he heard the riders approach. His face took on a puzzled expression when he saw the riders accompanying the wagon. Sudden recognition dawned and he grabbed for his pistol.

'Goddamn it, you got gall coming riding in here.' He looked with some wonderment at the driver of the wagon. 'Well done, Bert, looks like you brung in the gang all by yourself.'

The three riders sat their ponies too exhausted to protest. It fell to the wagon driver Bert to come to the rescue.

'Herbert, you put away that there pistol. You're pointin' it at the wrong people.'

A crowd was gathering. They stared with some curiosity at the newcomers.

'Hell, Bert, them's the fellas as busted outta jail and shot up Mr Miller's house.'

'Herbert, you ain't got the brains of a gnat. These fellas was the ones as was wronged. The man you want on the end of that gun is Miller — Granville Aloysius Garrett Miller. He employed that band of cut-throats to kill and rob. They're all in the back here. All dead 'ceptin' one and he's confessed to everything.'

It was too much for the lawman. His jaw gaped open and he stared in disbelief at the wagon driver. 'You crazy or something, Bert?' he said uncertainly.

'No, I ain't crazy. If anyone's crazy it's that pompous, no-good hypocrite as lives in that big house and puts on airs and graces for the benefit of us ordinary folk. If'n you won't take my word fer it then question that half dead fella as we brung in. He's the one remainin' member of the gang and he'll tell the truth of it.'

The pistol in the sheriff's hand never wavered. 'Bert, you been eating loco-weed.'

'Dang an' blast you to hell, Sheriff Dumbguts, I'm tellin' you the right of it.' Bert spluttered. 'That maverick up at that big house has bin hoodwinkin' us folk ever since he arrived here.'

'Bert, if'n you don't stop that language I'm gonna slam you in jail for abusing the law. Now you take that wagon down the morgue.'

'Lanny,' the sheriff called over his shoulder, 'collect these fellas' hardware. Then help me escort this bunch of owlhoots down to Mr Miller and settle this once and for all.'

There was nothing for it. The sheriff's deputy took their rifles and pistols and took them inside the jail.

'Right, you fellas, and you too, missy, turn them horses around and let's go a'visiting. Lanny and I are right behind you. Try and make a run for it and we'll blast you outta them saddles.'

31

Geraint opened the door to the sheriff's knock. He stood in the doorway almost blocking the entrance with his huge bulk.

'Geraint, tell Mr Miller we done caught us those escaped jailbirds.'

A wide smile broke across the black man's face. He stepped back from the door. 'Master will be pleased, Mr Sheriff. Take them down the kitchen. I'll fetch Master Miller straightaway.'

The sheriff and his deputy shoved Butch and Joe and Jessica down the hallway and into the kitchen. The fat cook was working away at her stove. The smell of the cooking almost overwhelmed the senses of the three captives. They hadn't eaten anything that day.

'Goddamn, if your cooking don't smell good.' Butch offered his most beguiling smile to the woman. His charm was somewhat spoiled by the blood and brain smeared on his face.

The cook stared nervously at the people crowding inside her kitchen. She was not used to men with guns invading her domain.

'Don't take no notice, Edna,' the sheriff assured her. 'The only food these fellas will be having is prison fare.'

The door opened and in swept Granville Aloysius Garrett Miller. 'Sheriff, you caught the miscreants. I do admire your courage and fortitude.'

The lawman straightened his shoulders and preened in front of the banker. 'I told you we would catch them. They've cooked up some sort of tale about you hiring some hardcases to rob and murder for you. I thought it best to bring them down here and let them confront you directly.'

Miller frowned at the three prisoners. 'You did right, Sheriff. Where are the men I sent to bring in these desperadoes?'

The sheriff shuffled his feet and looked discomfited. Before he could reply Butch spoke up.

'Your pet hounds are down at the morgue. Only one of them survived. It was him as told us about your cosy little arrangement with those killers. Couldn't stand your wife running away with someone. Had him sliced up to teach her a lesson.'

Miller's face tightened. 'Is he right, Sheriff, about those men being dead?'

'Sure thing, Mr Miller. Bert brung them back in his wagon. Those gunnies told me you gave them leave to bring in these escaped jailbirds. Ordered me to take my posse back to town. Next thing we know your hired hands is brung into town in the back of a wagon, deader than a bunch of hogs in the slaughter-house. If they'd a left me to it they might be alive now.'

'Your choice of expression is expressive if a little lacking in delicacy. I can see we have here some very dangerous men. And most brazen too, coming into town with an absurd story about my honesty. What to do with them is the problem.'

'You might as well confess now, Miller.' Joe was perching his backside on the back of a chair trying to ease his injured arm. 'It'll all come out at the trial.'

'Trial? I can hardly try myself. I happen to be judge in this here town. Sheriff, I suggest you leave these men in my charge. I will conduct an investigation into their crimes. When my enquiries have been concluded satisfactorily I will return them to your jurisdiction.'

'Ain't that a little irregular, Mr Miller?' The lawman frowned as he spoke. 'These are dangerous men. They should be behind bars.'

'Let me remind you, Sheriff, the last time these people were behind bars they walked free. I can't risk the same thing happening again. I suggest you go down the lockup and gather extra deputies. Take them in Good Eva

Arcadia and tell them the drinks are on the house. Come back in an hour or so with your deputies and we'll escort these killers to the jail. That way there is less risk of them absconding again.'

The lawman's face brightened. 'You say all the drinks is on the house?'

'Take as long as you like in there, Sheriff. Tell the men to drink up. It's all at my expense.'

As he was talking, the big black man Geraint and another servant were entering the room. They were armed and stared with hostile eyes at the captives.

The kitchen door to the outside opened and the young black girl who had befriended Jessica entered. She had paid the penalty for her kindness with a flogging. Now she stopped just inside the door. A look of fear came over her when she saw the crowd of men. She was carrying a basket of newly harvested vegetables. After a glance in her direction Miller's men ignored the girl.

'Sheriff, don't bother to come back

for us,' called Butch. 'We'll be killed while trying to escape.'

At a nod from Miller a man stepped forward and smashed his rifle into Butch's face. The force of the blow drove the cowboy back against the table. Only the sturdy construction stopped him from going down.

'Goddamn you, fella, I'll kill you for that!' Butch yelled. Blood dripped from a gash in his forehead. The guns in the room pointed at him and prevented him carrying out his threat. The cowboy had to content himself with glaring balefully at Miller.

'See, Sheriff, we have the situation under control.' Miller smiled reassuringly at the lawman while at the same time taking his arm and guiding him towards the door. 'Remember, take your time, and tell Max to serve you from my own personal whiskey bottle.'

It was slick and it worked. The sheriff was safely out of the way and would be busy for the next couple of hours swearing in his deputies and getting them liquored up at Miller's expense. When the banker turned his attention to the trio of dirty, bloodied and exhausted people in his charge he had a self-satisfied smile on his face. The smile did not reach his eyes as he stared at his prey.

'You people have caused me enough trouble. You've killed off my band of gunmen, the Lord only knows how. Those men were the best in the business. I would offer to take you into my employ in a similar role, but I have this feeling in my gut you would refuse to work for me. I get the distinct impression you don't like me. Every time we meet it seems to lead to violence. You've put my schemes at risk by spreading nasty tales about me. Now, just how to dispose of you so that fool of a sheriff will believe my version of events?'

32

Miller walked over to Jessica and gripped her chin in his hand. She flinched back from him and he backhanded her. With a gasp she stepped back. Miller grabbed a handful of her shirt pulled her forward again. It was too much for Butch. In spite of the man covering him with his rifle he threw himself forward.

The rifle swung and once more Butch was struck on his injured head. It was a vicious strike and Butch went down half rolling under the big kitchen table. Waves of dizziness swept over him and he groaned as he came to a rest on his back. He pulled himself over and attempted to rise on to his hands and knees. He could hear Miller still talking, ignoring Butch's attempt to get to him.

'It was fortunate I discovered you

were witness to the murder of your parents. Even though the men who did the deed are dead you might just persuade people to believe the killers were in my employ. Can't have such slander. Might ruin my good name. But you have given me an idea.'

Butch was on his hands and knees. He saw a pair of feet on the other side of the table. They belonged to the young servant girl, Ruth. She had put her basket on the table and the heaped vegetables shielded her actions.

She dropped the knife she used to peel and chop and using her foot edged the blade towards the man crouching under the table. Butch blinked in disbelief then quickly reached out and covered the knife with his hand. He began the laborious task of crawling from beneath the table.

'I think we will all take a trip out to the old Corley place. That's where my wife is being held hostage. Sheriff Johnstone will believe me when I tell him that in my anxiety to rescue my wife I made you take me to where you were holding her. During the rescue you attacked me and I had to kill you. Unfortunate, but would save us all a lot of bother.'

Joe was glaring at the banker, aching to get his hands on him. Geraint's bulk loomed beside him, grinning at him and almost willing him to do something foolish. The big black man had seen his fellow servant bludgeon Butch to the floor and was aching for similar violence against his captive. He was holding a large Navy Colt with the muzzle aimed at Joe's midriff.

Joe turned to watch his companion emerge from underneath the table. The cowboy seemed to have difficulty in moving. He crawled slowly and painfully forward. The man who was taking so much pleasure in hitting him now kicked him in the side of the head as his upper body came clear of the table. Butch toppled sideways groaning out loud. Joe's hands twitched as he watched his pal being punished so brutally. He turned to Geraint.

'Put that pistol down and face me like a man,' he gritted out — rage making him almost incoherent.

Geraint laughed, exposing large, yellow, uneven teeth. 'Make any moves against me and I'll gut-shoot you first and then beat you to death.'

Butch came off the floor fast. His tormentor was not expecting the quickness of the move. He was raising the rifle to hit his victim again.

Butch went in under the upraised weapon. He struck hard, driving his blade into the middle of the chest and up into the rib cavity. The man's eyes opened wide as did his mouth. His gasp of pain was harsh and very audible. Butch was gripping the man around the waist with his free hand as he buried the knife deep. He swung the man round to shield himself from possible bullets from Geraint or Miller.

The scuffle caught the attention of the big black man. He half turned towards the struggling pair. It was the opportunity Joe was seeking. He grabbed the Colt and at the same time smashed his fist into Geraint's face. Unfortunately it was his wounded arm he had to use and the pain shot into his shoulder, almost paralysing him.

Geraint instinctively pulled the trigger. The gun went off startling them both. Neither saw where the stray bullet went. Unfortunately it was aimed across the kitchen and entered the left breast of the big cook.

From the onset she had not moved from her position in front of the stove. The impact of the heavy slug pushed her back and her large buttocks pressed hard against the hot metal of the stove. She jerked forward and stumbled to her knees. Pressing her hand to the bullet hole in her chest she opened her mouth and began screaming.

On the other side of the kitchen Butch had grabbed the rifle from the guard's hand. There was no resistance for the man was dying on his feet. He slid from Butch's grasp and Butch now had possession of the rifle.

Miller jerked his head around to take in the struggles going on around him. With a swift movement he pulled Jessica close and snatched a revolver from a side holster.

Butch was bringing the purloined rifle to bear on the banker. He hesitated as he saw Jessica shielding him. Nearby, Joe and the giant Geraint struggled in grim silence for possession of the Colt. The big servant was slowly winning. He had the advantage of weight and the fact that he was not wounded. Joe, with his damaged arm, was at a desperate disadvantage as he struggled with his opponent.

Miller, taking in the fact that his bodyguards were unable to come to his assistance, let loose a shot at Butch. The bullet caught the cowboy in the side. Butch cursed as he felt the bullet rasp along his ribs.

He dropped to the floor and scrambled desperately beneath the large, wooden table. Miller sent another slug his way but this time hit the table leg. Seeing the state of his men with one down and one tied up fighting with Joe he made his decision. He brought up the revolver and clubbed Jessica. As she dropped to the floor he wrenched open the door and disappeared through it.

From underneath the table Butch saw his enemy getting away and fired after him. The bullet punched a hole in the door as it closed behind Miller. He turned his attention to the struggle going on between Geraint and Joe.

Joe was getting the worst of it. His opponent, seeing the blood oozing from Joe's upper arm from the bullet wound, was furiously pounding his big fist into the bloody upper arm. Joe held on desperately but his strength was waning. It had been a gruelling few days and the stressful events had taken their toll of the big man's considerable stamina.

Butch began the painful process of getting his wounded and battered body out from under the table and coming to his companion's rescue. He heard a grunt from the two fighters and looked up fearing the worst. For a moment he stayed where he was.

'My God,' he breathed.

Ruth had taken a hand in the struggle. Kitchen tools hung from hooks on the wall. Knives, mallets, cutters, grinders and graters — all ready to hand when the cook needed them. Ruth had chosen a meat cleaver. It was a heavy bladed tool with a maple handle worn smooth with use.

Butch watched with horrified fascination as the blade rose in the air. There was a thud as it struck the big black man in the back of the head. It was the sound a turnip would make if dropped to a hard floor. For the girl it was a supreme moment of revenge. Though her master had ordered the flogging it was Geraint that had applied the lash. Her back still hurt from that brutal punishment.

Under the impact of the blow,

Geraint's head jerked forward and butted Joe in the face. Blinded by the sudden pain as he was struck, Joe made one last supreme effort to wrench the gun from his opponent. To his surprise the grip slackened and suddenly he was in possession of the Navy Colt. He stared into the widening eyes of the giant he had been wrestling with. The man opened his mouth as if to protest. The eyes dulled — the mouth went slack and Geraint's head bent forward and nestled against Joe's chest.

Still holding the weapon he had struggled so desperately to gain possession of, a bewildered Joe watched his opponent sink to the floor. It was only when the black man knelt at his feet that he saw the cleaver embedded in the skull with the wood handle trailing down the stricken man's back like the tail of a coonskin hat.

He raised his eyes from the dying man and stared at the young girl. She was standing gaping down at her handiwork. With wide startled eyes she looked up at Joe. Then she bent over and vomited on the dead man. On the other side of the kitchen the cook's screaming had stopped. Her huge body rested against the front of the hot stove slowly roasting.

33

The big house was empty when they searched it. Miller had fled as had most of his servants.

'He'll go into town and bring the sheriff and his posse back with him,' was Joe's guess.

The searchers had armed themselves from the gunroom and were discussing options.

'In that case we better hightail it outta here,' was Butch's contribution. He looked pale and shaken. The side of his shirt was dark with blood from the fresh wound in his side. Blood had caked in his hair and face from the cuts in his scalp.

'Where to?'

Joe looked in no better condition. His arm was soaked in blood from the wound in his arm. Geraint's pounding had reopened the bullet wound and started the bleeding again. The two pals looked in no condition to take on a posse of armed men.

'I guess we havta go out to that Corley place Miller spoke about. That's where we'll most likely find the young girl as those fellas kidnapped from Empire Fastness Way Station. Miller said as that's where they were holding his wife. Trouble is, we don't know where it's at.'

'I can take you.'

The two battered men looked at Ruth. She huddled close to Jessica. The girls were striving to comfort each other. Both girls looked worn out with great circles beneath their eyes.

'I helped take food and clothes out there, but I only ever saw men. I never did see any females.'

'Mebby they didn't want you to see,' Butch observed. 'Anyway, I have to go. It's probably the only way to fulfil my promise to that fella I would find his sister.'

'You're right, Butch. But we'd need

fresh horses. Those mounts of ours is plumb wore out.'

'Where'll we find new mounts? We sure as hell can't go back in town.'

'We have stables here,' interjected Ruth. 'Master Miller has stable of good horses. His wife loved riding and they often rode out when she was here.'

Joe and Butch looked at each other.

'We might as well add horse-stealing to our list of crimes. They can only hang us once.'

'It looks like it's us two against the world.'

Their hands reached out and clasped.

Ruth led them to a little valley edging into the hills to the east of the place where they had fled from the posse. A small meandering creek lost itself in the distance. The sides of the valley were covered in purple and gold violets. The smell of pine wafted into the faces of the travellers as they rode into the valley. They paused and examined the old Corley place.

In the shelter of a few isolated trees

extending back into the valley, nestled the log cabin with a steep roof for snow to slide off. There was a corral with a couple of horses and a spacious barn. Other than smoke drifting up from the chimney there was no sign of life.

'Pretty a picture as I ever did see,' Butch observed as they looked on the peaceful scene. 'Fella could run a few head of cattle here and horses. Build it up to make a good living.'

'I guess,' Joe said wistfully. He was imagining bringing his wife here to live. Their child and any subsequent children would grow up strong and healthy in such an environment. He sighed deeply. His wife was back East and he reckoned she was lost to him forever. The further they progressed in this land the more outside the law they seemed to stray.

'You two girls stay hid while Butch and I go down and give the place the once over. We don't know if'n those killers left a guard.'

As they neared the cabin they could

see a man busy harnessing two horses to a carriage. He had his back to the riders as they walked their horses into the yard. Huddled in the front seat inside travelling rugs were two women. No one took any notice of their approach.

'That must be the guard. Mebby he's getting ready to return the females to Coventree,' murmured Butch.

The ride over had been hard. His head felt peculiar and his eyes kept going out of focus. But he was determined to see this thing through.

Riding beside him, Joe clung grimly on to his saddle. He couldn't move his wounded arm. The pain had been bearable up until it had been hammered by Geraint's big fist. The pounding had bruised and inflamed the wound. Now it felt as if a red-hot poker was being jabbed into the hole made by the bullet. Jagged streaks of pain radiated out from that side of his body. Joe wanted to slide to the dirt and lie there in the hope the pain would ease.

But he knew he must be there to the bitter end. Butch and he had come this far. They would complete this task together.

The man by the carriage turned and in his hand was a large nickel-plated revolver. He was smiling grimly at the two men on the horses.

'Thanks, boys, for bringing me my horses. I needed a couple of spare mounts. It was thoughtful of you to deliver them for me.'

'Miller!'

The two friends stared in dismay at the banker. Joe had a shotgun taken from the gunroom back at Miller's house. Because he was virtually one-handed he was caught with the weapon wedged into the saddle bucket.

Joe had his Remington pistols strapped to his waist. He had been reaching for one when Miller forestalled him.

The two battered men sat atop their mounts staring blankly at the unexpected sight of Miller. They had imagined the banker back in Coventree

284

organizing the posse to come for them. Now here he was, getting ready to make a getaway and it looked as if he was taking the women with him.

'Let the girl go, Miller,' Joe called. 'She's nothing to you.'

Miller smiled grimly at the man atop his mount taking note of the pain-etched features of the big man.

'I think not, my friend. I can't take a chance of leaving any witnesses. Now if you just throw down those weapons and then step carefully down from those horses I'll be on my way as soon as I tie them to the back of this wagon.' Imperiously he gestured with the gun. 'I don't want to harm the horses by shooting at their riders.'

The two friends glanced at each other. They realized there was no option but to comply. The banker had the drop on them. Reluctantly they drew their weapons and tossed them into the yard.

'Now get down and lie in the dirt.'

It was painful and frustrating to obey

but they were helpless in the face of that revolver pointing in their direction.

Miller was so engrossed in the two riders he did not see one of the women rise from her seat in the carriage. He was smiling triumphantly at the two men.

'I had a good little racket going till you two came along. I was able to pass information about banks and shipments of money and gold to my men. I used to call them Miller's Raiders. We amassed a nice little fortune. They kept their share here.' Miller tossed his head backwards indicating the carriage. 'When I leave here with my beloved wife I'll have enough to start up again somewhere else.'

They watched Mrs Miller shrug out of the travelling rug. She was wearing a dress in a heavy dark-green brocade. With unsteady hand she reached out and plucked the whip from its brass socket. Experimentally she dangled the whip, swinging it back and forth. With a sudden flick of her arm she swung viciously at the man holding the pistol.

With a crack the thong wrapped round the banker's face. He screamed out as the leather cut into the soft tissue of his eye. As he staggered forward he put his hands to his face.

The leather thong came free and the woman swung the whip round again readying for another strike. Joe threw himself upon the discarded shotgun. His shoulder jarred and for a moment he was paralysed with pain. With his good arm he kept scrabbling for the gun.

Beside him, Butch, more used to working with animals from his life as a cowboy, yelled out and swiped his mount across the withers. The horse jumped wildly and ran forward. Miller, half-blinded, could see only the shape of the horse charging towards him. He brought up his pistol. Before he could fire the startled animal was upon him. As he was knocked to the ground Miller screamed again and the terrified horse reared.

The banker, seeing the danger, tried to roll aside. Sensing the man beneath him, the horse tried to swing itself to the side to avoid trampling him. Unfortunately they both went the same way. Hoofs came down. There was a sickening crack of iron-shod hoof striking bone and Miller stopped screaming.

As the horse skittered aside, the banker's body could be seen twitching in its death throes. The horse wheeled and raced from the yard. No one was in a fit state to stop it. A woman's hysterical sobs was the only sound to break the peace of that little valley.

★　★　★

Butch and Joe stood beside the buggy. Ruth sat in the driving seat holding the reins. In the rear seat Jessica was sitting with her arm around a pale-faced youngster. Standing with the two men was the woman who had used the whip on Miller.

'Mrs Miller, there's no way in which we can thank you for what you done,' Joe said.

The big man towered over the woman in the green dress. She smiled up at him wanly, her face pale but composed.

'It's me that owes you. My husband was an evil man. It took a long time for me to discover just how evil. If you men hadn't come along who knows how long he might have carried on destroying people's lives.'

'What'll you do now?' Butch asked.

The woman smiled sweetly at the cowboy before replying. 'I'll go back to Coventree. Maybe I can make some reparation for all the trouble my husband caused. I'll try anyway.' She gestured towards the girls in the buggy. 'I'm hoping these girls will let me make amends for their wrongs. What are your plans for the future?'

The two men looked at each other.

'Ma'am, we ain't got any future,' Joe answered morosely. 'Officially we're escaped convicts. We just havta keep on going.'

Impulsively she reached up and taking Butch's face in her hands, kissed him. She did the same with Joe. They helped her up into the buggy.

'If you two change your minds there's always a place for you. I will need strong men to help me run Miller Holdings.'

Joe shook his head. 'Someday they'll come looking for us. You'd only get in trouble for harbouring two fugitives.'

Not looking at the people in the buggy Joe reached out and whacked the horse across the rear end. The vehicle lurched forward taking the women out of the yard.

'Let's go, pal. They'll be sending someone out to fetch Miller's body. We'd better be long gone.'

The two men mounted, stiff and sore from their many injuries, then rode slowly into the little valley.

'How you holding up, Joe?'

'I've this horrible feeling if'n Sheriff

Patterson had delivered us to the penitentiary like he should've, the last few weeks woulda been a whole lot pleasanter.'

'I guess. Where you reckon on heading now?'

'I've a mind to head for Mexico. Might be safer there seeing the law don't stretch over the border. What about you?'

'Maybe I'll head for California. I have this hankering to get me a sight of the ocean.'

'Mmm . . . there's an ocean down off the Mexican coast . . . '

They rode further into the valley, their voices fading into the distance. The purple and gold violets carpeting the slopes blazed with iridescence in the hot sun and peace fell gently in that remote place.

THE END

We do hope that you have enjoyed reading this large print book.

Did you know that all of our titles are available for purchase?

We publish a wide range of high quality large print books including:
Romances, Mysteries, Classics
General Fiction
Non Fiction and Westerns

Special interest titles available in large print are:
The Little Oxford Dictionary
Music Book, Song Book
Hymn Book, Service Book

Also available from us courtesy of Oxford University Press:
Young Readers' Dictionary
(large print edition)
Young Readers' Thesaurus
(large print edition)

For further information or a free brochure, please contact us at:
Ulverscroft Large Print Books Ltd.,
The Green, Bradgate Road, Anstey,
Leicester, LE7 7FU, England.
Tel: (00 44) **0116 236 4325**
Fax: (00 44) **0116 234 0205**

SILVER GALORE

John Dyson

The mysterious southern belle, Careen Langridge, has come West to escape death threats from fanatical Confederates. Is she still being pursued? Should she marry Captain Robbie Randall? The Mexican Artiside Luna has his own plans . . . With gambler and fast-gun Luke Short he murders Randall's men and targets Careen. Can the amiable cowboy Tex Anderson and his pal, Pancho, impose rough justice as with guns blazing they go to Careen's aid?

CARSON'S REVENGE

Jim Wilson

When the Mexican bandit General
Rodriguez hangs Carson's grandfa-
ther, the youngster vows revenge,
and with that aim joins the Texas
Rangers. Then as Carson escorts
Mexican Henrietta Xavier to her
home, Rodriguez kidnaps her. The
ranger plucks the heiress from the
general's clutches, and the youngsters make a desperate run for the
border and safety. Will Carson's
strength and courage be enough to
save them as he tries to get the
better of the brutal general and his
bandits?